YA
534
LAM

SOUND
More Than What You Hear

Christopher F. Lampton

ENSLOW PUBLISHERS, INC.

Bloy St. and Ramsey Ave.   P. O. Box 38
Box 777   Aldershot
Hillside, N.J. 07205   Hants GU12 6BP
U.S.A.   U.K.

Copyright © 1992 by Christopher F. Lampton

All rights reserved.

No part of this book may be reproduced by any means without the written permission of the publisher.

Library of Congress Cataloging-in-Publication Data

Lampton, Christopher.
    Sound: more than what you hear/Christopher F. Lampton.
       p. cm.
    Includes bibliographical references and index.
    Summary: Explains sound and discusses such topics as how we hear, ultrasound, and sonar.
    ISBN 0-89490-327-6
    1. Sound—Juvenile literature. [1. Sound.] I. Title.
QC225.5.L35 1992
534—dc20   91-22331
                                                                         CIP
                                                                          AC

Printed in the United States of America

10 9 8 7 6 5 4 3 2 1

Illustration Credits:
American Airlines, Inc., 38; Dennis Bailey, 12, 13, 17, 21, 26, 28, 32, 33; Korg U.S.A., Inc., 70; National Marine Fisheries Service, 79; National Portrait Gallery, Smithsonian Institution, 43, 44, 52; Official U.S. Navy Photograph, by Caroline Kiehner, 82; Panasonic, Inc., 49, 53, 55, 61.

Contents

	Introduction	4
1	Sound and Energy	8
2	Hearing Sounds	19
3	Sound and Information	30
4	Sound on the Go	40
5	Sound Recording	51
6	New Sounds	67
7	Seeing With Sound	77
	Glossary	88
	Further Reading	94
	Index	95

Introduction

What is sound?

That's a pretty easy question, isn't it? Sound is what you hear. It is information that enters your ear. It is . . . it is . . .

Alas, these are the kinds of definitions that raise more questions than they answer. Sure, sound is what you hear. But what is hearing? Yes, sound is information that enters your ear. But what form does that information take? How does it get into your ear in the first place? Where does it come from? Where does it go?

These are tough questions. Maybe you know the answer to some of them, but can you answer all of them?

That's what we hope to do in this book—answer any questions that you may have about sound: what it is, where it comes from, how it works. We'll look at how sound travels through the air, what happens to it when it enters your ear, and how sounds are created in the first place.

Just as importantly, though, we'll look at the technology of sound. In the nineteenth century, inventors began to discover ways to transmit sound over long distances, even to record sounds so that they could be played back at a later date. We take this technology so much for granted these days that it's hard to understand how miraculous it seemed a little more than a century ago, when inventions such as the telephone and the phonograph were brand new, as close to the cutting edge of technology as 32-bit microcomputers and high-resolution video game machines are today.

In some ways, the history of sound technology is the history of information processing—the changing of information from one form to another. The first sound recording and transmitting devices used a form of information processing called analog technology. We'll explain what that is in a later chapter of this book. Modern sound recording and transmitting devices are starting to use a much more advanced form of information processing called digital technology. We'll talk about that later in this book too.

Some people believe that the transition from analog technology to digital technology is one of the most important developments in information processing in this century. Why it's important will also be discussed later.

To give you some idea of what to expect and to help you organize your reading, here's a brief outline of the chapters that follow:

CHAPTER ONE: *Sound and Energy*. What is sound? How is it created? These are two of the questions that are answered in this chapter as we explore the relationship between energy and sound waves to see how sound waves travel from place to place. You'll also learn about the various parts of a sound wave, the speed at which sound travels, and the reason that people once believed an airplane could never travel faster than the speed of sound.

CHAPTER TWO: *Hearing Sounds*. What makes the whole subject of sound interesting is that we can *hear* it. How are we able to hear it? In this chapter, we'll see what happens to a sound wave when it enters your ear and what the shape of a sound wave has to do with the way it sounds inside your head. We'll also talk about such interesting sound phenomena as the Doppler effect and resonance.

CHAPTER THREE: *Sound and Information*. From the point of view of human beings, the most important thing about sound is that it carries information. But how does the information get into the sound? What form does that information take? We'll look at speech and music—two of the most important forms of sound information—and at noise, which is sound without information.

CHAPTER FOUR: *Sound on the Go*. Sound can travel fast, but it can't travel far. Many of the cleverest inventors of the last 150 years have searched for ways to make sound travel over longer distances than it normally would—even around the world and through outer space. We'll look at the development of the telephone, the telegraph, and the radio, three inventions that allowed sounds to boldly go where no sounds had ever gone before!

CHAPTER FIVE: *Sound Recording*. What if you want to hear sounds that were made yesterday or the day before—or even many years ago? If you're lucky, somebody recorded those sounds. But how can sound be recorded? In this chapter, we'll look at methods for recording sound, from Edison's original phonograph to cassette tapes to compact discs and even digital audio tapes. Even more importantly, we'll look at the difference between analog recording and digital recording—and see why computers have become increasingly important in the recording and transmitting of sounds.

CHAPTER SIX: *New Sounds*. Computers give us a surprising new ability. We can create sounds that don't exist in the "real" world. Musical synthesizers can imitate existing musical instruments or create whole new styles of music. Voice synthesizers can imitate the human voice itself—and voice recognition machines can listen to human speech and come very close to understanding it.

CHAPTER SEVEN: *Seeing With Sound*. We usually think of our sense of hearing as being very different from our sense of sight. But it is possible to use sound to do many of the things we ordinarily do with our eyes, literally to "see" with sound. Animals such as the bat and the dolphin do this all the time. And sonar allows submarines to navigate through the darkest of waters. We'll see how sonar works—and how it could one day be the deciding factor in a major war.

We'll cover all of these subjects and more in this book. If you're curious about sound, sound recording, sound transmission, or any other subject that has anything to do with sound, we hope you'll find the answers to your questions in the pages that follow.

1

Sound and Energy

Most of what we know about the world around us we learn in one of two ways: we see it or we hear it. We also learn through touching, tasting, and smelling, of course. But seeing and hearing are our most powerful senses. We learn more and learn faster through these senses than through all of our other senses put together.

Of the two, sight is the more powerful sense. Seeing is believing, the old saying goes. Our sense of sight tells us so much about the world around us that sometimes it seems as though it is the only sense we need. Yet even when we cannot see, we can still hear, and the "picture" of the world that comes to us through our ears is a rich one.

When you lie in bed at night, for instance, you can see only shadows. Yet you can still hear the world around you: the sound of traffic on the street; the patter of footsteps in the next room; the tinkle of laughter from a neighbor's house or apartment; the whir of a fan or air conditioner; the rattle and throb of a furnace or heat pump; the barking of a dog or the screeching of an angry cat.

When you have a conversation with another person, the words that you hear become more important than the things that you see. When your best friend tells you what happened to her the day before, her words are as important as the smile on her face (though the smile tells you a lot too). When your gym teacher explains the rules behind a new game or sport, you'd better listen carefully—or you may end up with a volleyball in your face.

And where would we be without the sound of music? A world without music would be much the poorer. Although it isn't necessary to hear music in order to survive, or even to get along in the world, it sure is a lot of fun.

This book is about sound: what it is, how we hear it, what we can do with it. Over the next several chapters we'll take you on a grand tour of that part of the world that we can hear and show you just how important your own sense of hearing can be.

Sound Waves and Energy
Sound is a kind of wave, not unlike the waves that roll across an ocean beach or ripple along the surface of a pond. A wave, in turn, is a way in which energy gets from one place to another.

Energy is what makes things move. It comes in two forms. We say that something has kinetic energy if it is actually moving. We say that it has potential energy if it could start moving with a minimum of effort.

A book sitting on a high shelf, for instance, has potential energy. If you bump into the shelf, the book will move all the way to the floor at a pretty fast clip. Once the book is on the floor, however, you must give it kinetic energy—that is, you must actually make it move—by picking it up and putting it back on the shelf.

There are other forms of energy, such as thermal (or heat) energy and electric energy, but these are actually specialized forms of kinetic energy. Electric energy, for instance, is the kinetic energy of the extremely small particles called electrons. Thermal energy is the kinetic energy of the particles called atoms and molecules that make up all ordinary matter. (When we say that something is hot—that is, has thermal energy—we mean that its molecules are moving around more than usual.)

Chemical energy is a kind of potential energy found inside molecules. When molecules containing chemical energy are broken apart into smaller molecules or atoms, the chemical energy is converted into other forms of energy. Usually it is converted into heat, but it can also be converted into kinetic energy and light. A rocket, for instance, is propelled by the chemical energy in its fuel. The heat and light of a wood fire comes from the chemical energy in the wood itself.

Energy never actually goes away. It just changes from one form to another. When the book falls off the shelf, for instance, its potential energy changes to kinetic energy. When it hits the floor, the kinetic energy of the fall becomes heat energy, making the book and the floor underneath it slightly warmer than they were before. And when you raise the book back to the shelf, the kinetic energy of the lifting motion becomes the potential energy that the book has while sitting on the shelf.

When you pick up a pebble and hold it above your head, you are giving the pebble potential energy. And when you let go of that pebble so that it falls back to earth, the potential energy is converted into kinetic energy. If the pebble falls into a pool of water, much of the kinetic energy of the pebble is transferred to the water itself—and becomes waves.

Water waves have much in common with sound waves. Because they are a little easier to understand than sound waves, we'll talk about water waves for a moment before we talk about sound waves.

When a falling pebble strikes the surface of a still pond, it forces the water to move aside slightly to make room. The water becomes bunched up, forming a tiny raised ring around the point where the stone breaks the surface. Gravity pulls this ring back down, causing a slightly larger ring of raised water to form around the first ring. This ring, too, is pulled back down by gravity, forming a still larger ring.

This ever-growing ring of water moves outward from the point at which the stone fell, propelled by the kinetic energy it received from the stone.

This moving ring of water is a wave. Usually, several such rings radiate—move outward in all directions—from the point at which the stone falls before the stone loses all of its kinetic energy to the water. As these rings grow larger and larger, their kinetic energy is spread out over a wider and wider area. The waves grow shallower and shallower until they disappear altogether.

If the waves strike something else along the way, such as an object floating in the water, they give some of their kinetic energy to that object. Sailors in small boats trapped in the waves (or wake) created by a big boat know that the kinetic energy of a wave can give them quite a violent buffeting.

Water waves are called transverse waves. The water itself is moving mostly up and down, while the wave—the pattern of motion in the water—moves sideways.

There are several important terms we use in describing water waves that we will also use later in describing sound waves. For instance, the highest point the water reaches above its normal level is called the crest of the wave. The lowest point to which the water falls below its normal level is called the trough. Usually, the trough is as far below the normal level of the water as the crest is above that level.

The distance from one crest to the next crest (or from one trough to the next trough) is called the wavelength of the wave. The number of waves that pass a given point in one second is called the frequency of the wave. The closer together the waves are or the faster they are moving, the higher the frequency. The farther apart the waves are or the slower they are moving, the lower the frequency.

We usually measure the frequency of a wave in cycles per second, or Hertz (abbreviated Hz; named for the nineteenth century German physicist Heinrich Hertz [1857–1894]). If one hundred wave crests passed a given point in one second, we would say that the wave had a frequency of 100 Hz.

The actual height of a wave is called its amplitude. When the crests of two different waves meet, their amplitudes are added together, producing a supercrest with the combined amplitude of the two crests. When a crest with an amplitude of two inches meets another crest with an amplitude of three inches, for instance, the result is a crest with an amplitude of five inches. This combining of waves is called wave interference.

If the trough of one wave meets the crest of another wave, on the other hand, they subtract their amplitudes, forming a much smaller crest or trough. When a three-inch crest meets a two-inch trough, for instance, the result is a one-inch crest. When a two-inch crest meets a four-inch trough, the result is a two-inch trough. And when a four-inch trough meets a four-inch crest, the result is perfectly flat water. The waves cancel each other out.

Sound Waves

Water waves move across the surface of water. Sound waves, on the other hand, move right through the middle of things. Sound waves can

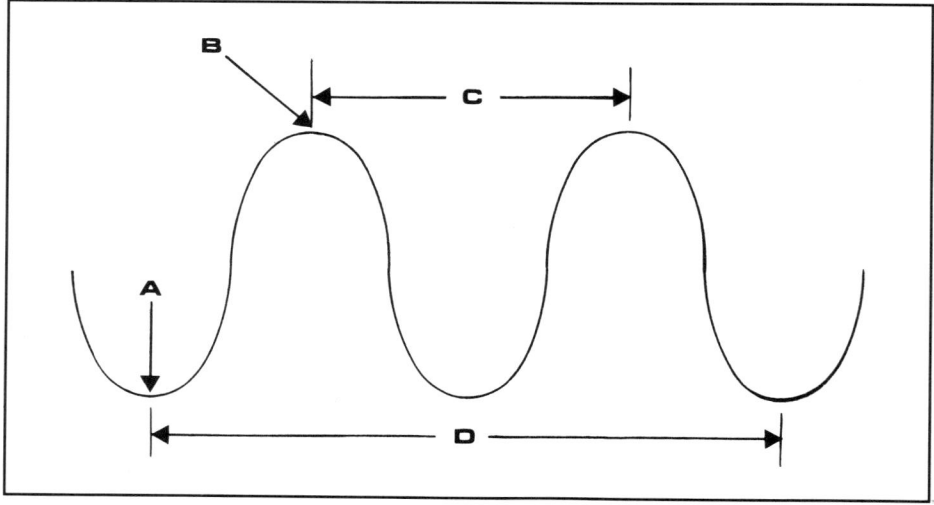

The attributes of waves: A–trough, B–crest, C–wavelength, D–frequency.

move through water, they can move through brick walls, they can even move through the earth itself. Human beings, however, live neither underwater nor inside the earth. We live in air. So, when we speak of sound waves, we are usually speaking of waves that travel through air.

Waves in air are caused by vibration, that is, by things that move back and forth very rapidly. Usually, an object vibrates because something has pulled it out of its normal position, giving it potential energy that moves it back into its normal position with such force that it moves right back out of position again.

An example will make this concept clearer. A guitar string vibrates when you pull it out of its normal position, using the kinetic energy of your finger to give the string potential energy. We say that this plucked guitar string has potential energy because the moment you let it go it is going to move back into its normal position.

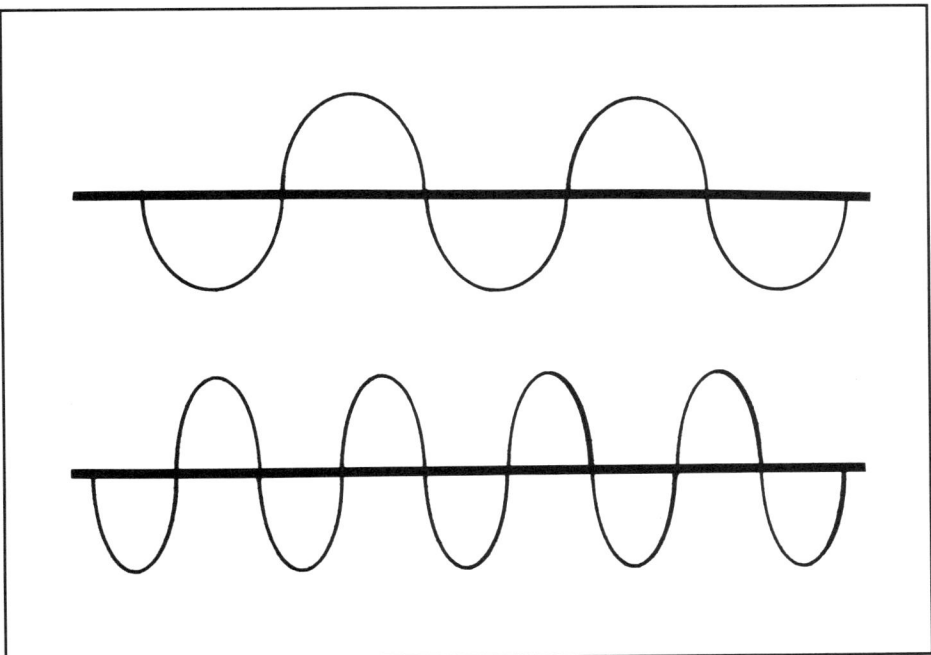

Two sets of wave frequencies. The more sets of troughs and crests, the higher the frequency.

And, indeed, when you let go of the guitar string, the potential energy is immediately converted into kinetic energy, and the string snaps powerfully back toward its normal position. So powerful is this potential energy, in fact, that the guitar string shoots right past its normal position until it goes almost as far to the other side, as though it were being plucked in the opposite direction. Once again, the string has potential energy, which converts back into kinetic energy, snapping the string back toward its normal position.

The string will keep overshooting its normal position until all of the kinetic and potential energy has been converted into other forms of energy. Some of this energy becomes heat energy. (Yes, the guitar actually gets warmer while it is being played.) And some of it becomes sound.

A guitar string is ordinarily surrounded by air. Like everything else on our planet, air is made out of tiny particles called atoms, some of which join together into the groups of atoms called molecules. The molecules that make up the air move around freely, not sticking to one another the way the molecules in, say, a brick do. That's why we can walk around through air almost as though it isn't there, instead of running into it as though it were a brick wall.

Vibrating objects such as guitar strings produce sound waves in air. As the guitar string vibrates in one direction, it passes some of its kinetic energy to the surrounding air molecules. The air molecules move more closely together (becoming compressed,) but when the guitar string snaps back in the other direction, they spring apart again (becoming decompressed). The kinetic energy of these air molecules moves outward from the vibrating guitar string in all directions, compressing and decompressing the air in a rapidly expanding compression wave or sound wave.

Like a water wave, the sound wave has crests and troughs. The crests of the sound wave are the points at which the air is the most compressed. The troughs of the sound wave are the points at which the air is the most decompressed. And like a water wave, the sound waves have an amplitude. Instead of representing the height of the wave, however, the amplitude of the sound wave is the difference in the compression of the air between a crest and a trough.

When the crests of two sound waves come together, their amplitudes add up to form a supercrest, with the combined amplitude of the two waves. As we will see in the next chapter, such a supercrest would sound very loud indeed! When the crest of one sound wave meets the trough of another, on the other hand, they can actually cancel one another out completely—producing silence!

Sound waves can travel through water and even solid matter in much the same way that they travel through air. But they cannot travel through a completely empty vacuum. Outer space is very, very quiet.

When a guitar string vibrates, the speed at which it vibrates determines the frequency and wavelength of the sound wave. The faster it vibrates, the smaller the wavelength and the higher the frequency. The more slowly it vibrates, the larger the wavelength and the lower the frequency. The greater the distance across which the string vibrates, the greater the amplitude of the sound wave.

The Speed of Sound

Like anything else that travels, sound takes a certain amount of time to get places. The speed with which sound travels through air depends on how quickly the air molecules respond to vibrations. The speed, in turn, depends on the temperature of the air. Cold air molecules respond to vibrations more slowly than do warm ones, so sound travels more slowly through cold air than through warm air. When we talk about the speed of sound, we are usually referring to the speed at which sound travels through air at 68 degrees Fahrenheit (20 degrees Celsius). At that temperature, sound moves through air at 1,130 feet (344 meters) per second.

Because it takes sound roughly five seconds to travel one mile, you can easily calculate how far away a flash of lightning is. The light from the lightning flash reaches you so quickly that it takes almost no time at all. By counting the seconds between the time you see the flash and the time you hear the thunder, then dividing the seconds by five, you can tell how far away the lightning is. For instance, if it takes fifteen seconds to hear the thunder, then the flash is three miles away. If it takes four seconds to hear the thunder, then the flash is four-fifths of a mile away. If you see the flash and hear the sound almost at the same time, then the lightning just missed you!

The different speeds that sound travels can cause interesting effects. During a temperature inversion, when the temperature of the air above the ground is higher than the temperature near the ground, the top part of a sound wave can move at a different speed from the bottom part. The sound wave will actually bend back toward the ground. Because temperature inversions often happen at night, sounds will sometimes seem to travel farther at night than during the day, with the sound wave rising into the air, then bending back toward the earth some distance away.

Sound, as we mentioned in the last chapter, can travel through other substances besides air. It can travel through water and even through solid steel. The speed with which sound travels through these substances is usually faster than the speed with which it travels through air because molecules of water and of steel respond more quickly to vibrations than do molecules of air.

In the 1940s, airplanes were first built that could fly close to the speed of sound. For a time it was believed that no airplane could fly faster than the speed of sound because the molecules of air would be unable to get out of the way in time to let the airplane pass through. Rather, the molecules of air would build up in front of the airplane until they formed a nearly solid wall, against which the airplane would be smashed to pieces. But in 1948, test pilot Charles "Chuck" Yeager became the first person to "break the sound barrier" by flying an airplane faster than the speed of sound. His airplane did not break into pieces. Today, of course, there are airplanes that fly several times the speed of sound. These are called supersonic ("beyond sound") aircraft.

An interesting effect occurs when an airplane passes the speed of sound. At the moment it breaks the "sound barrier," the airplane is moving at the same speed as the sound waves that it is producing in the air as it passes through. The wave crests that were racing ahead of the plane when it was moving slower than sound are now moving along with the plane, piling up in front of it. Just as the amplitudes of two wave crests in a pond add up to form a supercrest, these "trapped" sound waves add together to form an extremely loud sound wave, which we call a sonic boom.

If there were nothing more to sound than a wave passing through air, then it wouldn't be very important to us. We would hardly even notice that it was there. What makes sound important is that human

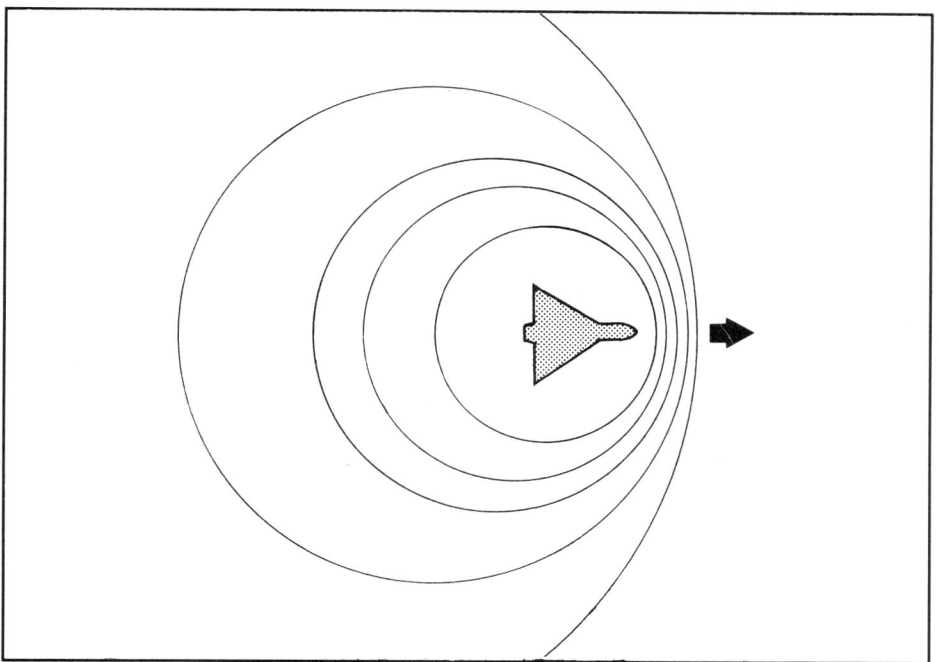

Breaking the sound barrier. As an airplane approaches the speed of sound, the distances between the sound waves it produces decrease. The waves pile up until the airplane reaches the speed of sound, when all the sounds are released in a sonic boom.

beings (and most other animals) have evolved special organs called ears that let us hear sounds. And that brings us to yet another definition of sound: Sound is something that you hear inside your head.

In the next chapter, we'll look at how you are able to hear sounds, and we'll see what the frequency and amplitude of sound waves have to do with the way that sound actually, well, sounds.

2
Hearing Sounds

To human beings, the most important thing about sound is that we are able to hear it. And we can hear it because we have ears.

The job of the ear is to turn the kinetic energy of sound waves into chemical and electrical energy inside the human brain. It does this job in two steps. First, it must capture the sound waves and focus them into a narrow passage. Then it must convert them into other forms of energy.

Sound in the Ear

The first step is performed by the outer ear, the part that you can see. The most obvious portion of the outer ear is the earflap, the shell-shaped piece of skin attached to the side of the head. The earflap acts like a funnel, capturing sound waves and directing them into a tiny tube-shaped passageway called the meatus (pronounced mee-AHT-us), which you can see inside the earflap. (Be careful about putting your fingers or other objects inside the meatus to explore it; if you aren't gentle, it's actually possible to damage the ear.)

At the end of the outer part of the meatus is a flat membrane of skin, stretched taut like the surface of a drum. And, in fact, we call this membrane the eardrum (or tympanic membrane). The sound waves captured by the earflap travel down to the meatus until they strike the eardrum. When the compressed part of a sound wave reaches the eardrum, it forces the membrane to move inward. After it passes, the decompressed part of the sound wave allows the eardrum to pop back out. But when the next compressed part of the sound wave hits it, it moves in again. In effect, the sound waves beat against the eardrum, similar to the way a drummer beats on a real drum.

When the sound waves strike the eardrum, they cause it to vibrate in exactly the same fashion as the vibrating object—a guitar string, for instance—that created the sound wave in the first place. If the guitar string is vibrating rapidly, then the eardrum vibrates rapidly. If the guitar string is vibrating slowly, then the eardrum vibrates slowly. If the guitar string is moving through a relatively long distance as it vibrates, then the eardrum moves through a relatively long distance (though obviously it can't move more than a fraction of an inch or it would be shattered. Unusually powerful sound waves can, in fact, harm the ear.)

On the other side of the eardrum are the middle ear and the inner ear, where the kinetic energy of the sound wave is converted into electrical and chemical energy. The middle ear is a kind of channel for moving the vibrations caused by the sound wave from the eardrum to the inner ear. It acts as both a safety buffer and an amplifier, protecting the inner ear from really loud sounds and making weak sounds loud enough to hear.

The middle ear consists of a small chamber full of air, in the middle of which are a series of bones called the auditory ossicles. It is the auditory ossicles that carry the sound vibrations of the eardrum into the inner ear. They are made up of three bones, called the malleus ("hammer"), incus ("anvil") and the stapes ("stirrup"), which are shaped more or less like the objects that they are named after. The malleus is attached directly to the eardrum and transmits the vibrations of the eardrum to the incus, which amplifies the vibrations—that is, makes them larger. If the vibrations are too large already and damage may result, muscles inside the middle ear change the positions of the eardrum and auditory ossicles, so that the vibrations will no longer be amplified. This system isn't perfect, however, and damage to the inner ear can still result from loud sounds.

At the other end of the auditory ossicles, the stapes is attached to another membrane of skin called the oval window (or fenestra ovalis). The vibrations from the eardrum travel through the incus into the stapes and from there directly to the oval window, which now vibrates at the same beat as the eardrum and the air itself. At this point, the vibrations enter the inner ear.

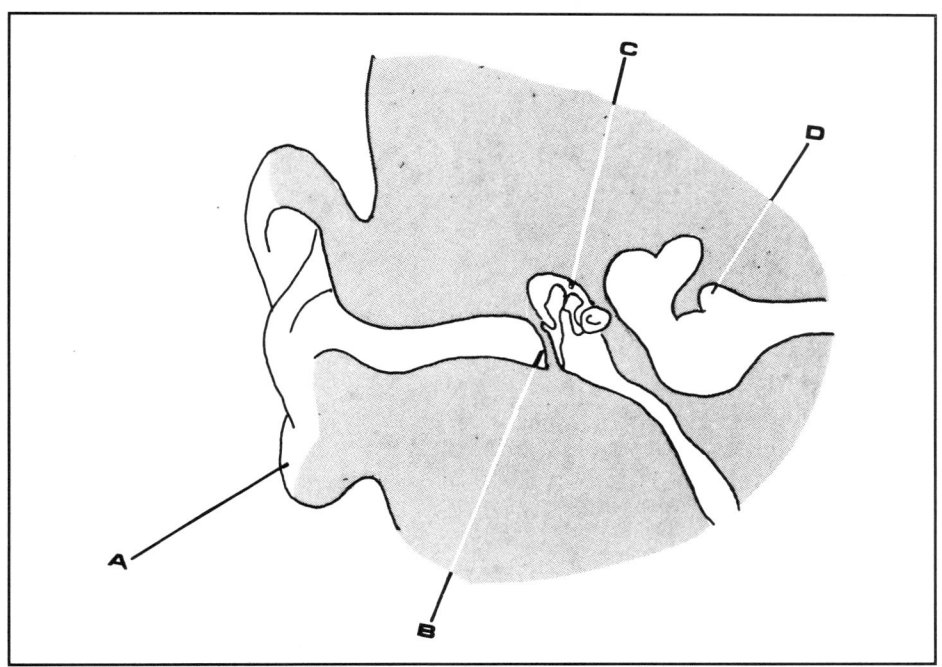

The structure of the human ear: A) ear flap; B) ear drum; C) middle ear including stapes, malleus, and incus; D) inner ear.

Once inside the inner ear, the vibrations wander through a complicated maze of passageways and tiny compartments full of fluid. As they wander through this labyrinth, the vibrations are sorted out by frequency, with rapid vibrations ending up in one part of the inner ear and slower vibrations ending up in another part. These sorted vibrations are detected by tiny hairs, which activate nerves that convert the vibrations into the electrical and chemical signals that travel into the brain.

What happens inside the brain is not yet fully understood, but the end result is that we "hear" the sounds inside our heads. Different kinds of vibrations produce different kinds of sound.

Because we have two ears, it is possible for us to tell from what direction a sound is coming. This process is called binaural ("two ears") hearing. Our brain compares the sound from both ears and determines which sound is louder. If the sound is louder in one ear than in the other, then the sound must come from that direction. By tilting our head slightly, we can locate the source of the sound very precisely.

There are many different kinds of sounds: loud ones and soft ones, shrill ones and deep ones. What is the difference between the sound waves that produce these different sounds? What gives a sound its characteristic loudness and pitch?

Loudness

When you create water waves by throwing a pebble into a pond, those waves rise a certain height above the normal level of the water. How high they rise depends on the force with which the pebble hits the water. The harder the pebble hits, the more energy it gives to the wave—and the higher are its crests. The height of the wave, as we saw in the last chapter, is called the amplitude.

In the same way, the more energy you put into plucking a guitar string, the more compressed the air will be in the compressed part of the wave (and the less compressed the air will be in the uncompressed part of the wave); the amplitude, in other words, becomes greater. This increase in energy makes the sound louder, because it makes your eardrum beat harder. The less energy you put into plucking the guitar string, the less compressed the air will be and the softer the sound will be.

As a rule, then, we can say that the more energy contained in a sound wave, the higher will be its amplitude and the louder its sound. The less energy, the softer the sound.

We measure the loudness of sound with a unit called the bel, named after Alexander Graham Bell, the inventor of the telephone. Because even a single bel represents a rather large difference in loudness, it is customary to use a tenth of a bel, or decibel (dB), for most measurements of loudness. A sound of 0 dB would be just barely audible, while a sound of 85 or 90 dB is loud enough to cause pain or even damage to the ear. Surprisingly, quite a few familiar sounds are louder than 90 dB. A motorcycle without a muffler, for instance, produces a loudness of about 100 dB. A jet plane, heard up close, produces about 110 dB. And a rock band can produce as much as 120 dB, which is why rock music has been known to damage the hearing of listeners and band members alike!

Fortunately for the health of our ears, loudness decreases with distance. The farther you are from the source of a sound, the softer the sound becomes because the energy in the sound spreads out over a larger and larger area as the sound wave moves outward from its source. The portion of the sound that reaches your eardrum, therefore, has much less energy in it and is unable to make your eardrums vibrate as hard.

The loudness of a sound falls off very quickly with distance. You might think that if you moved twice as far away from the source of a sound, then it would sound half as loud. Actually, it would sound one-fourth as loud. And if you moved four times as far away, it would sound only one-sixteenth as loud. Eventually, you would be so far away from the sound that you wouldn't be able to hear it at all. The energy of the sound would be so low that it would not be able to make your eardrums vibrate.

Although differences in loudness are caused by differences in the energy of the sound, a sound that is twice as loud as another sound doesn't have twice the energy of the other sound. In fact, it has ten times the energy of the other sound. Our ears magnify the differences between very soft sounds and shrink the differences between very loud sounds. Thus, we can hear a much wider range of sounds than we would otherwise be able to hear.

Pitch

The difference between a low, rumbling sound wave and a high, shrieking one is called the pitch of the sound. A low, rumbling sound is said to be low-pitched. A high, shrieking sound is said to be high-pitched. The energy of the sound wave has nothing to do with pitch. Differences in pitch are differences in the frequency of the sound.

The frequency of a wave, you will remember, is the number of wave crests that pass a given point in one second. In a sense, your ear "counts" the number of crests that strike it every second and your brain uses this information to determine if the sound is high-pitched or low-pitched. The more crests that strike your eardrum per second, the higher the pitch that you hear. The fewer crests that strike it, the lower the pitch.

Because sound always travels through air at the same speed (as long as the temperature doesn't change), the frequency of the sound is determined by the distance between wave crests, that is, the wavelength. The longer the distance between crests, the fewer crests will strike your eardrum every second. The shorter the distance between crests, the more crests will strike your eardrum every second.

As a rule, then, we can say that the shorter the wavelength of a sound, the higher pitched it will sound when it reaches your ear. The longer the wavelength of a sound, the lower pitched it will sound when it reaches your ear. The human ear can hear sounds with frequencies ranging from about 20 Hz (20 wave crests a second) to 20,000 Hz (20,000 wave crests a second). Sounds with frequencies less than 20 Hz are called infrasonic ("below sound"), and sounds with frequencies greater than 20,000 Hz are called ultrasonic ("above sound"). Many animals can hear sounds in the ultrasonic range, which is why dog whistles can be heard by dogs but not by people. A typical dog whistle produces sounds with a frequency of about 30,000 Hz.

If we return to our example of the guitar string, we can see how the sound of the string can be made to sound high-pitched or low-pitched. The distance between two waves created by a vibrating guitar string depends on how long it takes the guitar string to complete a single vibration, that is, to swing back and forth around its normal position. The longer it takes the guitar string to complete one full vibration, the longer the wavelength and the lower pitched the sound. The time it takes a guitar string to vibrate is, in turn, determined by how much slack there is in the string and how long the string is. You can actually change the length of the vibrating area of a guitar string by pressing against the string with your finger, which is why the same guitar string can play musical notes of different pitches. And you can adjust the slack (tune the string) by tightening or loosening the tuners at the end of the string.

We use a similar method to make our voices higher and lower pitched when we are singing. By deliberately tensing (or relaxing) our vocal cords, we change the speed with which they vibrate and make the sound waves produced by our vocal cords higher (or lower) pitched.

The Doppler Effect
The pitch of a sound also depends on how we are moving relative to the object making the sound. You may have had the experience of riding in a car when a fire truck (or ambulance or police car) hurtles past, siren wailing loudly. As the fire truck comes toward you, the

sound of the siren is high-pitched and piercing. Yet, as it goes past you, the sound suddenly drops in pitch, becoming less shrill if not exactly mellow.

A change in pitch that depends on the motion of an object making a sound is called the Doppler effect, after the nineteenth century Austrian physicist Christian Doppler (1803–1853), who first explained why it happens.

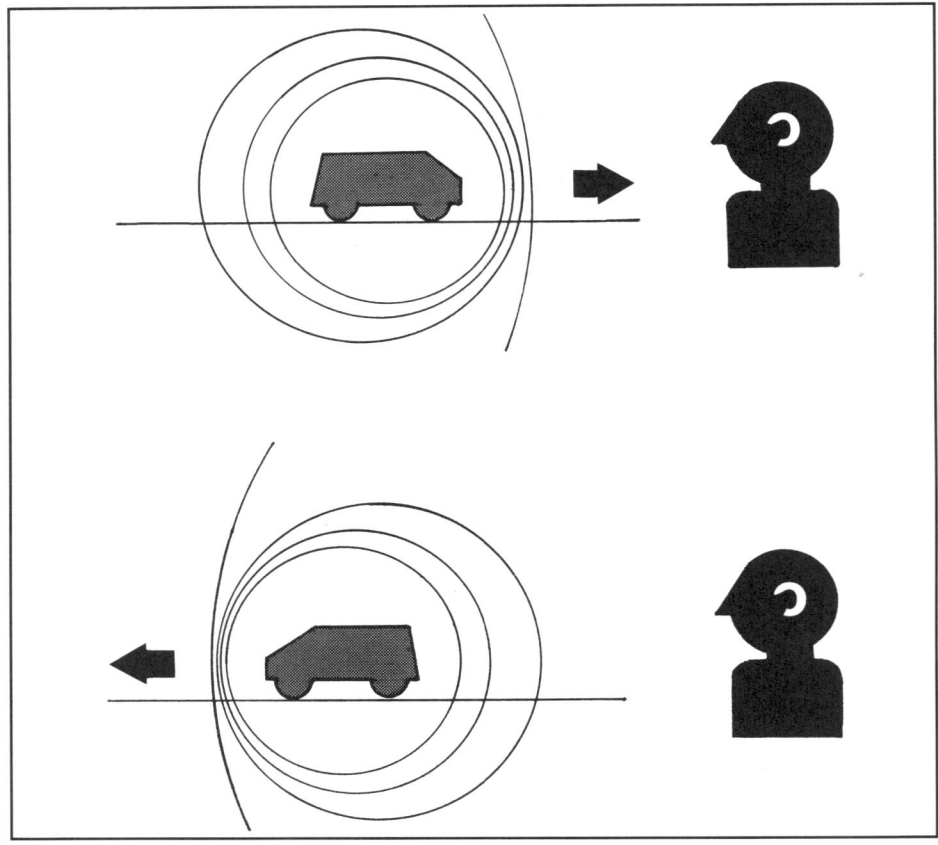

The Doppler effect is demonstrated here. As the source of sound moves closer, sound waves appear closer together creating a higher pitched sound. As the source of the sound waves departs, the sound waves appear further and further apart creating a lower pitched sound.

What causes the Doppler effect? Imagine that you are listening to a guitar being played by a musician perched atop a truck. As the truck moves toward you, the sound waves created by the guitar strings race ahead of the truck until they reach your ears. Because the truck and the guitar are moving toward you, each wave crest is produced when the guitar is slightly closer to you than when it produced the previous crest. The movement of the truck packs the wave crests closer together, making the wavelength shorter and the sound higher pitched.

After the truck passes you, however, it begins moving away from you. Each wave crest is now produced when the guitar is slightly farther away from you than when it produced the previous crest. The movement of the truck stretches the wave crests out, making the wavelength longer and the sound lower pitched.

The same thing happens if you are moving and not the source of the sound. If your friend is sitting on his front lawn playing a guitar and you ride past, the sound will be higher pitched as you approach him and lower pitched as you ride away.

Of course, the faster you are moving, the more dramatic the effect will be, which is why you don't notice the Doppler effect when you are walking unless a fast-moving vehicle hurtles past you.

Resonance and Reverberation

When sound waves strike a solid object, they can cause that object to vibrate, though usually not enough to make the object create sounds of its own. But certain objects, because of their shape or internal structure, will begin to vibrate strongly when they are struck with a specific pitch. This phenomenon is called resonance. When it happens, we say that the object is resonating. A resonating object will begin to produce sound waves of its own.

You may have observed this phenomenon for yourself. For instance, a large truck may rumble past your house or apartment and the windows will begin to vibrate in their frames, producing loud humming noises.

Or an object placed too close to the speaker of your stereo will start making noises when certain notes are played.

Not only sounds create resonance. Sometimes water pipes will generate harsh vibrations as water rushes through them at just the right speed.

When sound waves are trapped in a confined place, they will begin to bounce back and forth off the walls or other barriers that surround them. The result will be a series of echoes that cause the sound wave

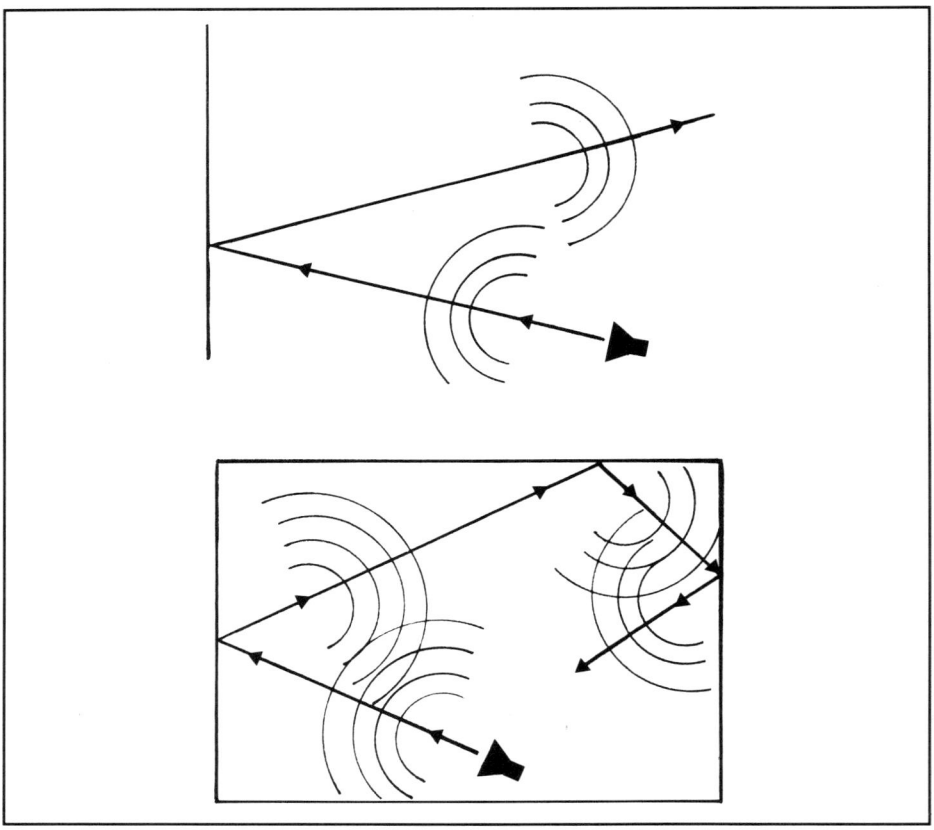

Resonance, or the change in a sound wave caused by bouncing off solid objects, is illustrated above. Reverberation, trapped sound continuously bouncing off objects, thus creating a echo, is shown in the bottom drawing.

to linger in the air much longer than it normally would. This series of echoes is called reverberation.

Musical instruments are often designed to use both resonance and reverberation to their advantage. Chambers inside instruments such as pianos and guitars are designed to trap sound waves and force them to reverberate, sustaining a note for seconds after it would normally die away. The materials out of which an instrument is made will resonate along with the music being played, and thus will amplify and enrich the sound of the instrument.

When we hear sound, we are hearing constantly changing pitches and amplitudes. These changing pitches and amplitudes are important because they carry information, knowledge about the world outside our heads and bodies. Sound carries information in many different ways, some simple and some complicated, as we will see in the next chapter.

3
Sound and Information

Sound wouldn't be nearly so important if it didn't tell you something about the world around you. The sound of thunder, for instance, tells you that it's time to get in out of the rain. The sound of your teacher's voice tells you that six divided by two equals three or that the Declaration of Independence was written in 1776. The sound of your mother or father angrily shouting your name tells you that you are in a lot of trouble.

Sound carries information. Information is anything that tells you something you didn't already know about the world around you. Almost every living organism on earth has the ability to receive information from the world around it. This ability allows organisms to adapt to changes in their environment. Even plants can detect changes in temperature or moisture or soil content. They can use this information to change the way in which they interact with the world.

Animals, because they can move around in a way that plants cannot, need a particularly large amount of information. Animals that eat other animals, for instance, need information about where those other animals are and where they are moving to, so that they can stalk them and capture them. In turn, the animals that these animals eat also need information so that they will know where the predators are and how to avoid them.

In time, more advanced animals gained the ability to create information and to direct it toward other animals. This process is called communication. No other animal is as good at communicating as human beings are and the most important form of communication between human beings is speech.

Speech

No one knows when human beings first became able to speak. Scientists who study the bones of our distant ancestors have long debated as to whether our close relative (and possible ancestor) Neanderthal man was capable of speech. Although studies of the skulls of Neanderthal, who lived about 30 thousand years ago, indicate that they had a slightly larger brain than modern human beings, the part of that brain used in speech seems to have been underdeveloped.

Whenever it arose, the ability to speak—and the ability to hear and understand speech—is one of the most remarkable abilities that humans have. Although animals can make sounds and can, in a few cases, even communicate with each other through sound, they cannot really speak in the way that humans do. Birds, for instance, claim territory through ritual songs. Apes apparently have a vocabulary of about a hundred signals similar to human words, but there is no solid evidence that apes can use these "words" to form sentences, as humans do. Human beings, on the other hand, can form a nearly infinite variety of sentences out of a vocabulary of thousands of words, and they can understand these sentences almost instantly when they hear them, even though they may never have heard those particular sentences before.

Speech begins in a part of the brain called the speech center, where sentences are formed. Speech is turned into sound in the throat and in the mouth, where we have several organs that are designed specifically for the creation of understandable sounds.

In the human throat is an organ called the larynx, which contains the vocal cords. When you breathe out, air passes through the larynx on its way to your mouth. When you tighten the muscles in your larynx, the air makes the vocal cords vibrate, and this vibration creates the sound wave that we call your voice. As we saw in the last chapter, you can control the pitch of this sound wave by tensing or relaxing your vocal cords.

The vocal cords by themselves cannot create speech. The rest of the job is done in the mouth, by the tongue and by the lips. Your tongue is one of the most versatile organs in your body. It can move into many different positions, changing the shape of the inside of your mouth and even blocking the flow of air. Your lips can also change the shape of your mouth and block the flow of air. By using these organs, you convert the sounds made by your vocal cords into the sounds of speech.

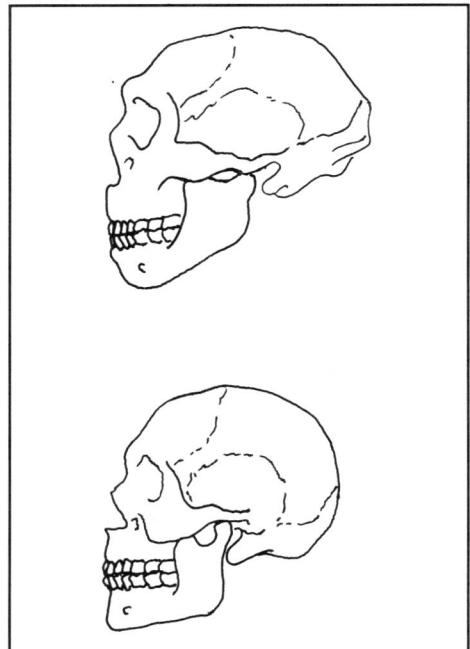

Though Neanderthals (top) probably had larger brains than modern humans (bottom), the speech making part of the brain was much smaller.

Speech experts divide the sounds of speech into different categories, depending on how the sounds are created in your mouth. The most familiar types of speech sounds to those of us who have never studied speech are the consonants and vowels.

Consonant sounds are created by stopping or slowing the flow of air in different ways. Some consonants require that you stop the flow of air with your lips. The sound of the consonant "p," for instance, is created by closing the lips until the air stops flowing, then opening them slightly so that the air bursts free abruptly. Try pronouncing such words as "pear" and "peach pit" and notice how they are created in your mouth. Your vocal cords almost completely stop vibrating while

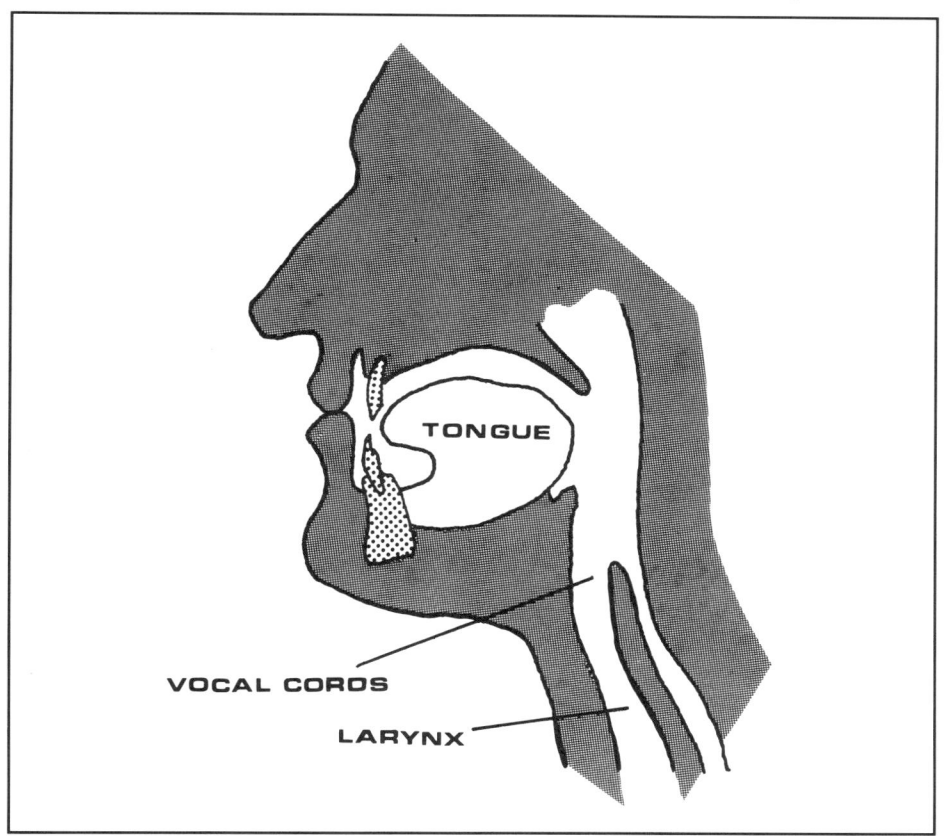

Key centers for the production of the human voice.

you pronounce a "p." This stoppage is especially obvious when the "p" is on the end of a word, such as "stop." The consonant "b" is also created by stopping the flow of air with your lips, but the vocal cords do not stop vibrating and the release of air is less explosive.

The consonant "d," on the other hand, is created by stopping the flow of air with the tip of your tongue against the roof of your mouth, then letting it burst out again; so is the letter "t," though the position of the tongue is slightly different. The "g" in the word "rang," on the other hand, is created with the back of your tongue against the roof of your mouth.

Letters like "s" and "f" are created by slowing down the flow of air, not blocking it. When pronouncing the "s" in "soup," for instance, you hold your tongue against the roof of your mouth so that the air rushes past it with a hissing sound. The "f" in "fudge" is pronounced by pressing your upper teeth against your lower lip and blowing air between them.

When you pronounce a vowel, you don't stop or slow down the flow of air as you do when you pronounce a consonant. Instead, you use your tongue and lips to change the shape of the inside of your mouth, which changes the quality of the sound from your vocal cords. Pronounce the names of the vowels "a," "e," "i," "o," and "u," and notice how you change the positions of your lips and the arch at the back of your throat as you create each sound.

The letters of the alphabet, in a sentence such as this one, represent the sounds of speech, but they don't do so consistently. The same letter can represent different sounds, depending on the word (or even the syllable) in which it is used. The letter "a," for instance, is pronounced one way in the word "cat" and another in the word "lace." To represent different sounds more consistently, experts on speech have developed so-called phonetic alphabets, where each character corresponds to one and only one speech sound. An example of such a phonetic alphabet can be found at the bottom of the page in most dictionaries, in the form of a pronunciation key.

The most remarkable thing about speech sounds, though, is that we can use them to carry information. By rearranging various sounds in different orders, we can represent almost any thought or idea that we wish. And anyone who hears those sounds, providing they speak the same language that we do, will know what we are talking about. Of course, it takes several years of training and study before we acquire this ability, but we are so young when we learn to do it that most of us can't remember a time when we weren't able to speak.

The Sound of Music
Perhaps the most fascinating form of information carried by sound is music. Even experts in music (musicologists) disagree as to the exact definition of music. And it is difficult to say exactly what kind of information music is. But anyone who has listened to music knows that it carries a powerful emotional message, a message that is difficult to put into words.

The sounds of music are much simpler than the sounds of the everyday world. The sound of a slamming door, for instance, is made up of sound waves of many different frequencies, mixed together in such a disorganized way that we shudder when we hear it. Musical sounds, on the other hand, are highly organized and very pleasurable to hear.

The simplest musical sound, a single pure note, is the sound of a tuning fork. When a tuning fork vibrates, it creates a type of sound wave that mathematicians refer to as a sine wave, a wave that rises and falls on a simple, repetitive curve. This note has a well-defined pitch, which a person with a well-trained ear can identify simply by hearing it.

Other musical instruments can play notes at the same pitch as a tuning fork, but they sound different to our ear than the tuning fork. Why do they sound different? Because the sound from these instruments is actually made up of several different sound waves with different frequencies blending together to form a sound wave with a single pitch.

The lowest frequency sound wave produced by a musical instrument is called the fundamental. The other sound waves produced by the instrument, called overtones, have frequencies that are multiples of the fundamental. That is, the first overtone has a frequency that is twice that of the fundamental, the second overtone has a frequency that is three times that of the fundamental, etc. We hear the fundamental and the overtones as a single note with the same pitch as the fundamental, but the overtones give the note a special quality. This special quality is called the timbre or tone color.

It is differences in timbre, created by differences in the amplitude of these overtones, that make an oboe sound different from a clarinet, for instance, or a piano sound different from an organ. In theory, if we could somehow adjust the amplitude of the overtones on a musical instrument, we could make one instrument sound much like another instrument.

Not all vibrating objects produce sounds where the overtones are multiples of the fundamentals. When the overtones are not multiples of the fundamentals, the result is a harsh and unpleasant noise. The various sound waves produced by the object interfere with one another, producing a complex sound wave in which the amplitude of the sound rises and falls rapidly, in a series of beats. Much of what we call noise, from garbage cans clanking in an alley to cats screeching at one another on the backyard fence, falls into this category.

Noise

Not all sounds are useful, enjoyable, or informative. Some sounds are just, well, noise. Noise can be thought of as junk sound, unwanted sound, even (in a few cases) dangerous sound. Usually it is sound that carries little or no information. Frequently, noise is discordant and harsh to the ear.

Noise is often a by-product of processes that aren't intended for the production of sound but that produce sound anyway. Examples include airplane takeoffs and landings, construction work, even parties. Sometimes one person's sound is another person's noise. A loud radio may be entertaining to the person who is listening to it, but to the people trying to sleep in the apartment next door it's just noise.

Unwanted sound can be thought of as a kind of pollution: noise pollution. Just as discarded chemicals can pollute our rivers and air, discarded noise can pollute our ears. At best, noise pollution is annoying. At worst, it can be dangerous.

According to some authorities, the amount of noise in the environment is increasing at a rate of roughly one decibel a year. Today, the average noise level in an average home is about 40 or 50 decibels. Of course, the precise amount of noise in your environment depends on what that environment is. If you live on a secluded farmhouse far from the hectic activities of a city, you are probably exposed to less noise than someone who lives in New York City . . . but you are still exposed to noise.

As we saw in the first chapter, very loud sounds can actually damage your ears. Even if you don't notice such damage right away, it can accumulate over time. Sources of damaging noise include airplane takeoffs as heard from a nearby vantage point, unmuffled motorcycle engines as heard by the rider, and rock music from a loudspeaker, either heard at the concert or on a particularly powerful stereo system. Extremely loud noises—150 decibels, say—can cause immediately noticeable damage, even deafness.

Scientists are only just now beginning to realize that the dangers of noise pollution extend beyond damage to the ear. Excessive noise can actually affect the way that blood travels through your arteries, restricting its flow so that your heart has to beat harder and your lungs have to pump more air. It can also cause psychological problems, making people more irritable and less productive, leading to headaches, ulcers, even allergic reactions.

What can be done about this pollution? In many instances, citizen groups have been formed to force airports and other sources of high decibel noise to relocate away from populated areas. But this sort of solution isn't always possible . . . or wise. Moving an airport away from one community may simply cause it to be built next to another community. In the end, somebody's ears will suffer. Pilots taking off from certain airports are told to take off and land away from populated areas, but this directive sometimes forces the pilots to make hazardous aerial maneuvers that endanger the passengers on the planes in order to save the ears of those on the ground.

Noises that might be considered acceptable during the day are often unacceptable at night, when people are trying to sleep. One way to reduce nighttime noise pollution is simply to shift noisy activity into the daylight hours. Once again, airports have commonly agreed to schedule their noisiest activities during waking hours. And construction work is rarely done at night. Ultimately, the best solution may be to adapt our technology to our need for silence. Airplanes, automobiles, and jackhammers can be redesigned to minimize the amount of noise that they produce. Mufflers reduce the noise produced by automobiles, for instance, as anyone who has ever heard a car

The sound of an airplane taking off can cause hearing damage.

driven without a muffler can attest. Unfortunately, making a machine run more quietly sometimes also makes it run less efficiently. This may be the price we pay for silence, however.

Perhaps the worst noise pollution occurs in the workplace. Some people work in noisy environments, and the constant exposure to noise can cause all of the reactions to noise that we described above, including hearing loss. And not just jackhammer operators run a risk of losing their hearing. Rock musicians commonly suffer from hearing damage because of their constant exposure to highly amplified sound. Unlike workers in some noisy areas, such as airport runways, rock musicians are not able to wear earplugs while they work. Peter Townshend, lead guitarist and songwriter for the 1960s and 1970s rock group The Who, suffered permanent damage to the nerves in his ear during his years of concert performing and was unable to play his trademark electric guitar during the group's late 1980s revival tour.

Long Distance Communication

As human beings, we commonly use the sounds of our voices to communicate. But in order to communicate with someone who is not currently in our vicinity, we need a way to get the sound from where we are to where he or she is. Finding a way isn't always easy.

Sometimes, as a substitute for talking to someone, we send letters. Writing gives us a chance to organize our thoughts and even to preserve them until a later time, but it isn't always quite the same as talking to a person directly.

For long-distance communication, we need a way to make sounds travel over long distances. Until the middle of the last century, there really wasn't any solution to this problem. Then, in 1844, a remarkable invention allowed sounds to travel over hundreds and even thousands of miles, and the world hasn't been the same since!

4
Sound on the Go

Sound travels fast, but it doesn't travel far. The energy of a sound, spreading outward in all directions like the surface of an inflating balloon, thins out quickly. Eventually, the sound becomes inaudible, that is, too soft for the human ear to hear. As you know, the distance that the sound can travel before it becomes inaudible depends on how much energy the sound had to begin with. Very loud, energetic sounds travel a lot farther than softer sounds with less energy. A gunshot can be heard much farther away than a whisper. (In fact, the whole point behind whispering is that it can't be heard very far away.)

The loudest sound in recent history was the explosion of the volcano Krakatoa in the year 1883. It was heard many thousands of miles away. But it is a rare sound indeed that can travel that far. Most loud noises travel a few miles at most, and a normal human voice can be heard only a few hundred feet away under the best of conditions, such as those in a public auditorium.

Sometimes you simply have to communicate with someone who is too far away to hear you. What do you do then?

The Many Forms of Information

One of the most remarkable things about information is that it can take many different forms, yet it still remains the same information. A person speaking French communicates using a completely different set of sounds from those used by a person speaking English, yet the information contained in those sounds can be exactly the same.

The information in sound is stored in a pattern of differing wavelengths and amplitudes, just as the information in a book such as this one is stored in patterns of differing letters, sentences, and paragraphs. If we could transfer the patterns in sound into another form that could travel great distances at great speeds and then transfer the patterns back into sound again, we would have a method of sending messages very far very fast.

In the mid-nineteenth century, a way was discovered. It involved converting the patterns in a sound wave into electricity, which travels at almost unbelievably fast speeds, so fast that it can travel around the world in less than a second. Electricity is the flow of tiny particles called electrons, which travel through certain substances called conductors much as water travels through pipes. It is electricity that makes light bulbs glow, air conditioners hum and heaters heat. Electricity accomplishes these things by carrying kinetic energy from place to place, just as sound carries energy from place to place. But electricity carries energy farther and faster than sound ever can. By translating the information in sound into electricity, we can send that information very quickly over long distances.

The Telegraph

The first person to develop an effective way to convert the information in sound into electricity was the American inventor Samuel Morse (1791–1872). With considerable help from a second inventor, Joseph

Henry (1797–1878), Morse developed the telegraph, a relatively simple device that uses a pressure-operated key to turn an electric current on and off. In this way, the sound of the key clicking against a metal pad could be transmitted electrically over a wire to a second telegraph many miles away, where electricity turns an electromagnet on and off, causing a second key to click.

How could a device such as this be used to carry information? Morse invented a special code that came to be known as the Morse code, which used the sound of a clicking key to represent the letters of the alphabet. For each letter, there was a series of clicks that represented that letter. A telegraph operator at one end of a telegraph system could send a message by tapping on the key, which could be interpreted by a second operator listening to the clicking of the telegraph key at the other end of the system.

In this way, the information contained in the pattern of clicking keys could be sent as far as electricity could travel over a wire. Morse's first telegraph system ran from Baltimore, Maryland, to Washington, D.C., a distance of more than thirty miles. In 1844, he opened this telegraph line for business. The first message that he transmitted on it was the sentence, "What hath God wrought?"

With the invention of the telegraph, it was no longer necessary to wait weeks or months for a written message to be carried hundreds or thousands of miles to a faraway person. The telegraph allowed messages to travel at the speed of electricity, which was fast indeed.

Still, the telegraph was an awkward way to convey information that would normally be contained in the sound of a human voice. For one thing, a telegraph can be used only by a trained telegraph operator, who knows the Morse code and can tap out messages at rapid speeds. Furthermore, the early telegraph systems were capable of carrying only one message at a time on each wire. The result was that there was often a long waiting period before a message could be sent. Also, sending a message was expensive.

Samuel F.B. Morse (1791–1872), invented both the telegraph and Morse code, the signal language used by telegraph operators.

The Telephone

How much nicer it would be if there was a way to carry the actual sound of a human voice over an electric wire. Then anyone, not just a trained operator, could send messages quickly over long distances. The inventor who provided such a method of transmitting the human voice (and other sounds) over electric wires was, of course, Alexander Graham Bell (1847–1922). His invention, later improved by Thomas Alva Edison (1847–1931), was the telephone.

The secret of the telephone lies in the so-called carbon microphone, a device that converts the pattern of frequencies and amplitudes in a sound wave into an electrical current. The carbon particles in a microphone are electrical conductors, which means that an electric current can travel through them. But the amount of electricity that can travel through the carbon particles at any one time depends on how

Alexander Graham Bell (1847–1922), inventor of the telephone.

tightly compressed the particles are. Compress the carbon particles and the amount of electricity passing through them increases. Decompress them and the amount of electricity passing through them decreases.

In a simple telephone, the microphone contains a collection of carbon particles with a thin plate, or diaphragm, pushing against them. Sound waves make this diaphragm move. The crest of a sound wave, for instance, pushes the diaphragm inward, pressing it against the carbon. The trough of a sound wave pulls the diaphragm outward, removing it from the carbon.

While the carbon is being compressed and decompressed by the diaphragm, an electric current is passing through it. When the carbon is compressed, the current increases (as described above). When the carbon is decompressed, the current decreases. In this way, the microphone translates the pattern of wave crests and troughs in the sound wave into a pattern of increasing and decreasing electrical currents. In a sense, the rising and falling sound wave is now a rising and falling electrical current.

This electrical current, in turn, can be carried over a wire, just as the electric current from a telegraph can be carried over a wire. At the other end of the wire, however, the current must be channeled into a telephone receiver. The receiver uses this increasing and decreasing electric current to power a magnet, which causes a second diaphragm to move inward and outward as the current increases and decreases. This diaphragm, in turn, causes the air around it to vibrate, in an exact reversal of the process by which the vibrating air in the microphone caused the diaphragm to move. A sound wave is created that is almost identical to the one that caused the microphone to vibrate at the other end. A person with an ear placed close to the receiver can hear this sound wave. By placing microphones and receivers at both ends of the telephone line, a two-way conversation can take place, with both participants able to talk to each other and to hear each other.

The principle of the telephone is also used in the device called the loudspeaker, which can be found in auditoriums, stadiums, classrooms, theaters, and many other public places. A loudspeaker is much like a telephone receiver. It contains a diaphragm that is made to vibrate by an electric current. However, the electric current carrying the sound information from a microphone to a loudspeaker is amplified—made stronger—to make the sound much louder than it would be otherwise. Soft sounds spoken into a microphone become loud sounds that can be heard over a large area when they come out of the loudspeaker.

Radio

The telephone allows us to send sounds, and therefore the information in sounds, anyplace where there are wires. In the more than a century that has passed since Bell invented the telephone, wires and cables carrying telephone information have been placed around most of this planet, even traveling beneath the ocean.

But it would be even more convenient if we could send the information in sound to places that wires cannot travel—into the air, for instance, or outer space. Such an invention was created in the late nineteenth century by the Italian electrical engineer Marchese Guglielmo Marconi (1874–1937). That invention is the radio.

Both of the devices we have talked about so far, the telegraph and the telephone, have converted the information in sound into electrical form and transmitted that sound through a wire that conducts electricity. To get away from wires, however, it was necessary for Marconi to convert sound into a form that could travel through empty space itself. The form he chose was electromagnetic radiation.

Electromagnetic radiation is a wave that travels through space itself, the way that sound waves travel through air and other substances. Light is a form of electromagnetic radiation, as are X-rays, microwaves, gamma rays, and radio waves. Like other kinds of waves, electromagnetic waves have a wavelength, a frequency, and an amplitude.

The form that electromagnetic radiation comes in depends on its wavelength. Visible light, for instance, is made up of several different wavelengths of electromagnetic radiation, with blue light representing one wavelength, red light another wavelength, and so on. (White light is made up of many different wavelengths of electromagnetic radiation jumbled together.) Our eyes are instruments for detecting these wavelengths of electromagnetic radiation—or, more specifically, for detecting and decoding the information carried by these wavelengths of electromagnetic radiation, a process we call vision or seeing.

Our eyes are not capable of seeing other wavelengths of electromagnetic radiation, and thus we do not tend to think of other forms of electromagnetic radiation as being light, though in a sense they are. Ultraviolet and infrared are also forms of electromagnetic radiation, as are X-rays (a form of "light" that can be used to see through solid flesh, among other things), microwaves, gamma rays, and so on.

Because electromagnetic waves travel through empty space, they can go just about anywhere that there is empty space. Some wavelengths of electromagnetic radiation can also travel through gases such as air, and a few can travel through water and even solid walls. Electromagnetic radiation also travels very, very quickly; in fact, it is the fastest thing in the universe. The speed of electromagnetic radiation is generally referred to as the speed of light, because light is the most familiar form of electromagnetic radiation. The speed of light is 186,000 miles (300,000 kilometers) per second. Nothing that we know of can travel faster than light.

Marconi's invention was designed along principles discovered earlier by the German physicist Heinrich Rudolph Hertz. It is a device for converting the information in sound into the kind of electromagnetic radiation that we now call radio waves and for converting it back into sound again after it has traveled where we want it to go (and often where we don't want it to go). Because radio waves do not need wires to carry them from one place to another, a radio signal can go places that the telephone does not (and, in many cases, cannot).

Marconi's first radio was crude compared to modern radios. It used a loop of electric wire with a gap in it that produced electromagnetic waves when the electric current leaped across the gap, creating a spark. (For that reason, the gap in the wire was called a spark gap.) The inventor attached a telegraph key to the wire, so that he could turn the electric current on and off, using the electromagnetic waves generated at the spark gap to send Morse code messages.

A few years after Marconi, the American inventor Reginald Fessenden (1866–1932) built a radio that converted sound waves into radio waves. He used a microphone to translate patterns of sound into an electric current, which he ran through a wire similar to the one Marconi used to produce electromagnetic waves. As the strength of the current increased, the amplitude of the electromagnetic waves produced by Fessenden's radio increased. As the current decreased, the amplitude of the electromagnetic waves decreased. Thus, the pattern in the sound waves was encoded in the amplitude of the electromagnetic waves. Because Fessenden's radio changed (or modulated) the amplitude of the electromagnetic waves, it came to be called AM (short for amplitude modulation) radio.

Just as an electric current in a wire or rod can produce an electromagnetic wave, so can an electromagnetic wave produce an electric current in a wire or rod. Thus, the electromagnetic wave can be converted back into electricity, which in turn can be converted back into sound much as in the receiver of a telephone.

A wire or rod that is used to convert electricity into a radio wave or to convert a radio wave back into electricity is called an antenna. Large antennas at radio stations create powerful radio signals that can travel over long distances. Radio receivers use smaller antennae to convert those signals back into electricity, which can then be converted back into sound.

Early Radio Broadcasts

The first radios were very crude and could carry only Morse code signals. For this reason, they were sometimes referred to as wireless telegraphs, or just wirelesses, for short. In 1901, Marconi himself made the first transatlantic radio broadcast, sending a brief Morse code message from Cornwall in England to Massachusetts in the United States. To do so, it was necessary for him to send his broadcasting antennae aloft in balloons, far above the earth's surface.

Fessenden made the first sound broadcast in 1906. It consisted of recorded music and Fessenden himself reading from the Bible and playing musical instruments. It was heard mostly by radio operators on ships along the East Coast of the United States.

Radio quickly became important as a method of sending emergency messages, as the sinking of the HMS *Titanic* in 1912 illustrated.

Today's tiny portable tuners are a great deal smaller than the receivers of 1906.

Although more than 1,500 lives were lost when the *Titanic* sank, many more were saved because rescue vessels arrived only hours later in response to a radio distress signal.

By the late 1920s, radio had become an important business. Regularly scheduled radio broadcasts featured musical performances, as well as short comedies and dramas. In fact, radio programming was much like the television programming of today. Radio programs included situation comedies, dramas, westerns, news, documentaries . . . and, of course, commercials. The three major television networks, **NBC** (the National Broadcasting Company), **ABC** (the American Broadcasting Company) and **CBS** (the Columbia Broadcasting System) all began as radio networks. And, in fact, the radio divisions of these networks are still active today, though they are overshadowed by their television counterparts.

Sending sounds over long distances has revolutionized the way that we communicate with one another. If you want to talk to a friend or relative who is far away, you don't have to travel to where they are. You just pick up a telephone. And if you want to know what the news is or to hear the latest hit song, just turn on the radio.

But radio messages vanish as quickly as they are produced. What if you want to hear yesterday's hit song and nobody is playing it anymore? Or if you want to hear a message from a friend all over again? What then? Nothing can bring back yesterday's sound waves once they have lost their energy and the last vibrations have disappeared.

Fortunately, it is possible to record sound waves so that yesterday's sound waves can be today's sound waves as well. The secret of sound recording was discovered in the late 1870s by a man some consider the greatest inventor of all time.

5
Sound Recording

There are some sounds that we want to hear more than once—music—for instance, or the dialogue of a good movie or TV show. We need a way to record these sounds, that is, to convert the information in these sounds into a more permanent form so that we can change it back into sound whenever we want to hear it.

Sound recording, in the form of the phonograph, was born rather abruptly in the late 1870s. The phonograph was the inspired creation of the great American inventor Thomas Alva Edison. Edison's phonograph (or gramophone) used a rotating cylinder covered with tinfoil to preserve the information in the sound.

How can sound be preserved on a foil-covered cylinder? Next to the cylinder, Edison placed a diaphragm attached to a needle. When sound waves struck the diaphragm, they caused it to vibrate, in the same way that they cause your eardrum to vibrate. The diaphragm, in turn, caused the needle to vibrate, just as your eardrum passes its vibrations to the delicate bones inside your ear. The needle then etched these vibrations into the tinfoil itself, while someone turned a handle that caused the cylinder to revolve around and around. The needle slowly moved along the length of the cylinder, creating a spiral-shaped groove that traveled almost the entire length of the tinfoil.

When the needle was forced to follow this groove a second time, the vibrations etched into the groove made the needle vibrate in almost exactly the same way as when it created the groove. The needle, in turn, caused the diaphragm to vibrate again, recreating the sound.

Although this system was crude compared to that used to create and play back modern phonograph records, it worked. The Edison system could be used to record most loud sounds, including music and the human voice, though no one was likely to mistake the recorded sound for the original.

Thomas Alva Edison (1847–1931) and the gramophone, forerunner of the phonograph.

Many improvements have been made in this system since Edison developed it. Several years after Edison invented his phonograph, a pair of inventors developed a new version that used a wax-covered cylinder, which produced better sound than Edison's tinfoil-covered cylinder. In 1904, the German-American inventor Emile Berliner (1851–1927) invented a new type of phonograph in which the sound was recorded in a spiral groove on the surface of a disc instead of on the surface of a cylinder. While the needle on Edison's phonograph had created a groove that became deeper and shallower as the sound wave rose and fell, the groove on Berliner's disc moved from side to side. To this day, phonograph records are created in the disc shape invented by Berliner.

Today, however, these records are made out of several different types of plastic that we refer to collectively as vinyl; hence the term

Modern vinyl albums record sound within a spiral groove. The needle of the turntable moves from side to side within the groove retracing the recorded sound wave.

vinyl recordings is sometimes used to describe the Berliner-style disc records. While early Berliner and Edison recordings were made by using a vibrating diaphragm to drive a needle, modern recordings use electricity to transmit sound information from the microphone to the device that records the sound.

In recent years phonograph records have begun to fall out of favor. Some experts have predicted that vinyl records may disappear completely by the turn of the next century. They are being replaced by two newer recording media: magnetic tape and compact discs.

Magnetic Tape

The term *media,* when used to describe a recording, refers to the form (or medium) in which the recording was made. Phonographs are one such medium for recording sound; magnetic tape is another.

A magnetic tape is covered with a semiliquid substance, called an emulsion, that contains within it tiny magnetic particles. The magnetic fields—the north and south poles—of these particles are pointed in all different directions when the tape is manufactured.

In order to record on a magnetic tape, the sound waves must first be converted into a rising and falling electric current, as we have described already in this and the previous chapter. This current is then used to generate a magnetic field. The recording tape is passed through this magnetic field, and the field causes the magnetic particles on the tape to line up all in one direction.

As the electric current rises and falls, the magnetic field generated by the current changes, too, and the manner in which the particles line up on the tape changes. In this way, the information in sound waves is converted first into a rising and falling electric current, then into a changing magnetic field, and finally into a changing pattern of lined-up magnetic particles on the surface of the magnetic tape.

To hear the sound recorded on a magnetic tape, we move the tape past a magnetic head that can detect the alignment of the particles on its surface. This magnet generates an electric current that is fed into an amplifier that in turn drives a speaker and reproduces the sound on the magnetic tape.

One obvious advantage of magnetic tape is that it is much easier to record on tape than on a vinyl disc; in fact, it can be done in the home with relatively inexpensive equipment. Most homes now contain the equipment, called a tape recorder for both recording and playing magnetic tapes.

Nowadays, magnetic tape is usually placed inside a tiny plastic package called a cassette. These cassettes are created and played in specially designed cassette recorders and players. Because they are simply snapped into the players and ejected at the touch of a button, these cassette devices are much easier to use than the earlier reel-to-reel tape recorders, which actually required that the user thread the

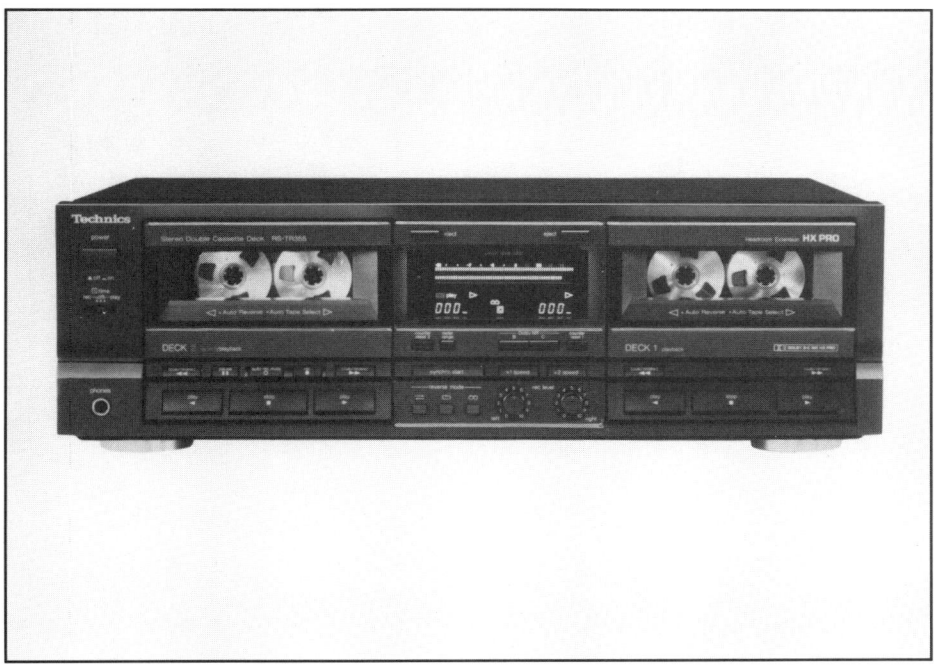

A cassette player recorder. This was the first means by which ordinary people could record sound in the privacy of their own home.

tape through a complicated series of wheel and gears before it could be played.

The ease with which cassette tapes can be used to record music and other sounds has been a source of consternation to executives of companies that sell prerecorded records and tapes because they fear that consumers will use tape recorders to make copies of records that they might otherwise buy. Despite this fear, however, the recording industry enjoyed greater sales in the 1980s than in any previous decade.

Magnetic tapes are also more compact and easier to carry and store than vinyl records. Their use has led to the popularity of small portable tape players that people can carry with them while exercising or walking to work or school. For these and other reasons, sales of prerecorded magnetic tapes surpassed sales of vinyl discs in the 1980s and have led to predictions that vinyl will disappear completely in the 1990s.

Another recording medium also came on the scene in the 1980s, one that has rapidly gained popularity and that some experts believe to be the recording medium of the future. In some ways, this new medium represents as significant a leap in the history of recorded sound as the invention of the phonograph itself, because it uses a brand-new method of storing sound information: so-called digital recording.

Compact Discs

Hold a vinyl record up to a good light and examine the spiral groove on its surface. The groove is no smoothly curved line, spinning neatly from the rim to the center of the disc. Rather, it is jagged and wavy, smooth for short stretches and then shaky for longer stretches. In fact, it looks a lot like a picture of a sound wave. And that is exactly what it is.

Where the sound wave rises, the groove in the surface of the record rises, too. Where the sound wave falls, the groove in the surface of the record falls. When the needle of a phonograph moves through this groove, it vibrates back and forth exactly as the groove moves back and forth, thus beginning the process of recreating the sound wave. (Actually, the groove in the record rises and falls in two different directions, both of them at angles to the phonograph needle. One direction contains the sound information for the right stereo speaker and the other direction contains the sound information for the left stereo speaker.)

When something is like something else in a certain way, we say that it is an analog of the thing. A model airplane is an analog of a real airplane, for instance. A landscape painting is an analog of a real landscape.

Because the groove in the vinyl record is so similar to the sound wave itself, we say that it is an analog of that sound wave. Thus, we refer to vinyl records as an analog recording medium.

Magnetic tapes are also an analog recording medium. The way the magnetic particles on the surface of the tape are arranged correspond exactly to the rising and falling of the sound wave itself. Similarly, the electric currents that carry the sound wave to the amplifiers and speakers in both magnetic tape recorders and phonographs rise and fall exactly as the sound wave they represent rises and falls. Thus, these electric currents are an analog representation of the sound wave.

Until the 1980s, most sound recordings were analog. But there is another way of representing sound waves: as a series of numbers or digits. When a sound wave is represented as a series of numbers, we say that it is represented digitally.

Here's a rough sketch of how sound waves are represented digitally:

First, we'll draw a picture representing a sound wave as a rising and falling line. This line represents the rising and falling density of the air as the sound wave passes through it. Underneath the rising and falling line, we'll add a straight line, which we'll call the baseline.

Now we'll add evenly spaced marks along the baseline, as though it were a ruler.

Finally, we'll add vertical lines stretching from each of these marks straight up to the curved line representing the sound wave. Each of these lines will be a different length, depending on how far above the baseline the sound wave is at that point. These lines measure the height of the sound wave as it passes over one of the closely spaced marks on the baseline.

Now, if we take a ruler and measure each of these vertical lines (in millimeters, say), we'll have a series of numbers representing the height of the sound wave at each of these points. And we could use these numbers to reproduce the sound wave, even if we had never seen a picture of the sound wave before, in much the same way as you create a picture by drawing lines between dots in a connect-the-dots puzzle. We have, in effect, represented a sound wave as a series of numbers.

For instance, the numbers describing such a sound wave might be 2, 4, 7, 12, 18, 20, 21, 19, 17, 14. . . . We can tell just by looking at the numbers that the wave rises and then falls again. We can then "connect the dots" to produce a rough drawing of the wave described by those numbers.

That's how digital recording works. The sound wave is first converted into a rising and falling electric current, as we described earlier. Then it's fed into an electronic device called an analog-to-digital converter, or ADC for short. The ADC samples the electric current at evenly spaced intervals (usually tens of thousands of times a second) and measures the strength of the current at each of these intervals. What comes out of the ADC is a second electric current, but this time the electric current represents a series of numbers that tells how strong the current was (and how "high" the sound wave was) at each of those intervals.

The numbers represented by the electric current leaving the ADC are all zeros (0s) and ones (1s), with a high voltage electric current usually representing the number one and a low voltage electric current representing the number zero. (It can be done the other way around, too, as long as it is done that way consistently throughout the whole system.)

Zeros and ones can represent any number we want if we use the binary numbering system. In binary, there are only two digits: 0 and 1. All binary numbers are made up of combinations of these two digits. Ordinarily, we count using the decimal numbering system, which uses ten different digits. For every decimal number, there is an equivalent binary number; for instance, the binary number 11011 is equivalent to the decimal number 27. The binary number 10011101 is equivalent to the decimal number 157.

Binary is the numbering system used inside all digital computers, including the personal computers you have probably used at school or in your home. By using high and low electrical voltages to represent binary numbers, we can build simple electronic devices to perform calculations on those numbers, adding them, subtracting them, and playing all sorts of fancy tricks with them. This is the secret behind not only personal computers, but also pocket calculators, digital alarm clocks . . . and compact discs.

An analog-to-digital converter converts an analog electric signal into a digital electric signal. A rising and falling electric current representing a rising and falling sound wave enters the ADC. The ADC measures the strength of the voltage a certain number of times per second and converts the measurement into a binary number. What comes back out of the ADC is a second electrical current, representing a series of binary numbers that describe the same sound wave, with high electrical voltages representing ones and low electrical voltages representing zeros.

The number of times per second that the ADC measures the sound wave is called the sampling rate. Compact discs are recorded with a sampling rate of 44,100 times per second. Thus, one second of sound on a compact disc is represented by 44,100 binary numbers. Although this may sound like a high sampling rate, there are critics of CD recording who say that it is not high enough. They point out that the sampling rate must be high enough to produce an accurate representation of high frequency sounds, in which the sound wave rises and falls many, many times per second.

To be precise, the sampling rate must be at least twice as large as the frequency of the highest pitched sound that is being recorded, so that the ADC can sample the wave once as it rises and once as it falls. If this is not done properly, the sound wave will be incorrectly reconstructed by the CD player. In many cases, an extremely high-pitched sound—even a sound too high-pitched for the human ear to detect—may be reconstructed as a very low-pitched one, a phenomenon known as aliasing. The result is a mysterious low-pitched hum in the recording that was not present in the sound being recorded.

Once we've used an ADC to convert sound information into a series of numbers representing the shape of the sound wave, we can record those numbers on the surface of a compact disc using a laser beam. The surface of the compact disc is coated with a silvery reflective substance, but underneath this surface is a dull, nonreflective interior. A strong laser beam can be used to cut tiny holes in this surface, exposing the nonreflective substance beneath. In compact disc terminology, these holes are called pits. The reflective surfaces around the pits are called lands. It is these pits and lands that we use to record binary numbers on the surface of the compact disc.

The length of a pit represents a sequence of ones and zeros called a channel code, according to a special coding system agreed upon by manufacturers of compact discs. Some of these channel codes represent the binary numbers produced by the ADC describing the sound wave

Once a compact disc has been recorded, it can be played back in a compact disc player. A beam of light (or a very mild laser beam) is trained on the disc's surface while the disc is made to rotate. Optical devices recognize the presence of pits and lands on the surface of the disc by noting the way in which they reflect the laser beam. A tiny computer in the player analyzes this information, deducing the shape of the sound wave described by the channel codes. The computer feeds this information into a digital-to-analog converter (DAC), which converts it back into a rising and falling electrical current representing that sound wave. This current is amplified and fed into a speaker, which produces the sound originally recorded on the CD.

Wow! That's a pretty complicated process! Why bother to do all this work when it's so much easier—in theory, anyway—just to represent sound with a groove on a vinyl record?

There are several advantages to recording music on a CD. One is that nothing more than a beam of light ever touches the surface of the disc. Therefore, the surface can be protected by a transparent plastic shield, which prevents it from becoming damaged during playing. Thus, it is expected that a CD will sound just about as good after ten or twenty years of constant playing as it does when it's new. That's not true of a vinyl record, where the needle that reads the sound

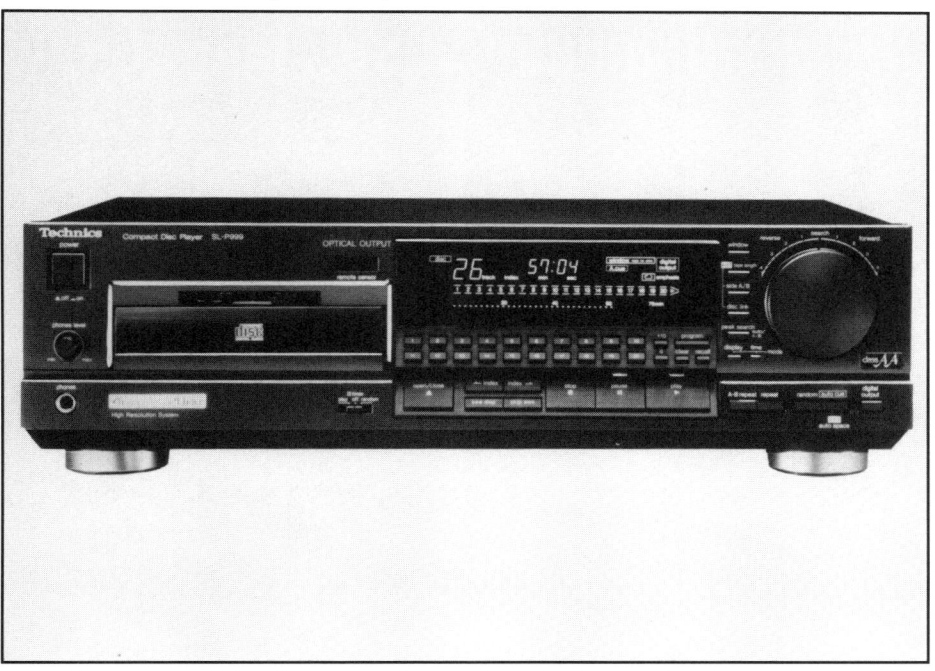

CDs are expected to replace vinyl recordings completely by the year 2000.

information from the groove actually wears down the groove every time it plays. Cassette tapes also deteriorate with age; the magnetic heads that read the tape tend to scramble the magnetic particles that hold the sound information.

But that's not the most important reason. Information stored in digital form can be reproduced more accurately (and inexpensively) than information stored in analog form. When we represent a sound wave as a rising and falling electrical current, we must be careful to reproduce that current at every point in our recording and playback system . . . and such reproduction requires sophisticated, expensive equipment. Even the slightest change in the electric current will give us a different sound wave and will lower the quality of the sound.

Digital systems, however, use only a high- and a low-voltage electrical current. (This is a slight simplification, but it captures the basic idea of digital recording.) It's hard to mess up such a simple representation, and so digital systems can be made from much less expensive equipment than analog systems and still produce excellent sound reproduction.

Furthermore, the channel codes on the surface of a compact disc contain more than just a description of the sound wave being recorded. They also contain error correction codes. As a result, even if the compact disc player makes a mistake in reproducing the electrical signal carrying the binary numbers (or if the factory made a mistake in producing the compact disc), the computer inside the player can detect the error and correct it! Such accuracy is not possible with analog recordings.

Still another advantage of digital recording is the precision with which recordings can be copied. When an analog recording is copied from one tape to another, there is always some loss of information. This is the reason that analog audio tapes recorded from other analog audio tapes never sound quite as good as the original. Digital recordings, on the other hand, can be copied perfectly because copying digital information is simply a matter of copying binary numbers, something that computers do exceptionally well. Unless something goes very, very wrong, a copy of a digital recording should hold exactly the same information as the original and should sound exactly the same when played.

Finally, the fact that the information is in digital form means that we can process it with a computer. For instance, the computer inside the compact disc player can (in theory) remove unwanted noise from the recording or change the quality of the sound to something more pleasing or even combine the sound from one recording into the sound from a second recording. We can even mix different kinds of information on the same disc. A few compact discs now feature pictures as well as music, though the pictures can be seen only by using special compact disc players that attach to televisions. In the future, compact discs may be available with full animation and video in addition to sound.

By now, you may well be convinced that digital recording is the wave of the future. And why stop with compact discs? Why stop with music recording at all? How about digital telephones? Digital radios? Digital television?

All of these things and more are being considered, and some are in active development. A digital telephone system, known as the Integrated Services Digital Network (ISDN), is already being put in place in cities across the United States. Instead of analog signals—rising and falling electric currents—in telephone lines, ISDN uses digital signals.

With a digital phone system, telephone calls could potentially sound as good as compact discs. And you'll be able to send any kind of digital information (faxes, computer programs) over your telephone just by plugging the phone jack into the proper electronic gadget. To some extent, of course, we can already do some things along this line. Computers can be hooked to the telephone, for instance, through a device called a modem. But with a digital telephone system, modems will no longer be needed. And the speed at which information can be sent will be many times faster than it is now. A number of special services are being offered in cities where ISDN has been installed, including Caller ID, which lets you see the telephone number of the person calling you while the phone is still ringing.

Digital radios and digital TVs are a little further down the road, but prototype systems for both have already been built. (In theory, ISDN can be used to send digital radio and television over telephone lines.) One day, probably within the lifetime of most of the readers of this book, almost all sound transmission and recording systems will be digital ... and sound will never have sounded so good.

Disc and DAT

A second medium for digital sound recording is the digital audio tape, or DAT for short. DATs work much like CDs, with sound being converted into binary numbers by an analog-to-digital converter, but with DATs the zeros and ones are recorded in the positions of magnetic particles on the surface of a tape. Thus, digital audio tapes not only sound as good as compact discs when played on a DAT player, but DAT owners can make digital recordings at home, of much better quality than conventional analog cassette recordings.

The most striking thing about digital audio tapes is that a DAT recorder can make copy after copy of a single tape without any loss of quality whatsoever. The copies sound identical to the original. With analog cassette tapes, each generation (copy of a copy) of a tape sounds inferior to the tape it was copied from, until (say) a fifth-generation tape is almost unlistenable. With DATs, a fifth-generation tape will sound just like a first-generation tape.

Much as the introduction of inexpensive analog tape recorders worried recording company executives, who feared that the home recording of tapes would cut into record sales, the introduction of DATs has raised the possibility of home recordings that are of equal quality to commercial recordings. The record company executives fear that the commercial record industry could be devastated.

This seems an unlikely occurrence. Nonetheless, it is possible for the owner of a DAT recorder to make perfect copies of the sound information recorded on compact discs. Not nearly perfect, but perfect. As we saw a moment ago, it cannot be done with analog recording media. But it is quite possible with digital media, because copying digital information involves simply copying numbers from one medium to another, something that computers and digital recording devices usually do flawlessly.

To prevent owners of DATs from recording CDs onto tape, DATs will be recorded at a different sampling rate from that used in CDs. The sampling rate, you'll recall, is the number of times per second that the analog-to-digital converter measures the strength of the electrical current representing the sound wave and converts it into zeros and ones. The sampling rate used in recording CDs is 44,100 times a second. DATs will probably record at more than one sampling rate, depending on the quality of recording you want and the amount of tape you want to use. However, most DATs will not record at a sampling rate of 44,100 per second. They will play recordings made at that sampling rate, so that they can play commercial recordings originally intended for compact discs, but only expensive commercial DAT equipment will record at that rate.

Therefore, it will not be possible to directly record—that is, to copy binary numbers—from a CD to a DAT recorder. It will still be possible to record from a CD to DAT, but it will be necessary to convert the digital sound on the CD into analog form before it can be re-recorded on the DAT, which will lower the quality of the recording.

In addition, commercially recorded DATS will use a special copy protection system that allows owners of DAT recorders to make a single copy of them.

The recording industry hopes that these safeguards will give people an incentive to buy CDs rather than try to record them on DATs. Nonetheless, it seems almost inevitable that some manufacturer will eventually bring out an inexpensive DAT recorder that will record at the same sampling rate used on CDs, despite the objections of recording industry executives. Whether such a machine will hurt the sales of CDs remains to be seen.

Vinyl records, magnetic tape, CDs, and DATs are ways in which existing sounds can be preserved for posterity. Sounds that are recorded digitally on CDs and DATs can even be altered by computer to sound better (or worse or just different) than they did before.

But digital sound offers us yet another possibility: the creation of sounds that never existed before. No longer is it necessary to build expensive musical instruments every time we want to create a new type of music. We can build our instruments inside computers as computer programs!

6
New Sounds

In the last chapter, we saw how sound information can be represented as a series of binary numbers in the same way that all types of information are represented in computers. We also saw that this system allows us to use computers to process the sound information, correcting errors in that information and changing it in ways that we find interesting and useful.

Let's take this idea a step further. In making and playing a digital recording, we convert a sound wave into a series of numbers and then back into a sound wave again. But what if we started with the series of numbers? What if we used a computer to create a series of numbers that represented an imaginary sound wave, then fed those numbers to a digital-to-analog converter to create the sounds themselves?

If we could do what we've just described, we could make new sounds, sounds of a type that have never been heard before on this planet. And, in fact, it has already been done. This process is called sound synthesis, and it plays an important role in the creation of music and other types of sounds.

Music Synthesis

The first important role played by sound synthesizers was in the creation of musical sounds. The first music synthesizers, developed in the 1950s and 1960s, were not digital but analog. We saw earlier how sounds can be converted into electrical currents, then back into sounds again; this is the way in which a telephone works, for instance. An analog synthesizer creates a rising and falling electric current, then converts it into a sound that has never existed before. This "new sound" can be amplified, played through a speaker, even recorded. An analog synthesizer can imitate the sounds of existing instruments or can create new types of musical sounds. Analog synthesizers, particularly the Moog synthesizer developed by inventor Robert Moog, were popular with rock musicians in the 1960s.

Analog synthesizers tend to be expensive, unwieldy, and not very flexible. To change the sound that an analog synthesizer makes, you must physically rewire the synthesizer. (A typical analog synthesizer has several "preset" sounds wired into it in the factory.) To change the sound of a digital synthesizer, on the other hand, you need to change only the computer program that generates the numbers that represent the sound, which is much easier than rewiring the synthesizer.

A digital synthesizer is a kind of computer, as well as a kind of musical instrument. The computer calculates the numbers that represent the sound to be synthesized; then those numbers are output to a digital-to-analog converter and converted into sounds.

How can a computer calculate a sound wave? In theory, this is a simple process. A computer programmer takes the information that scientists have learned about the nature of musical sounds and then programs the computer to produce the numbers that describe these sounds. In practice, it has proved not to be so easy.

Until the 1950s, it was believed that the overtones (as described in Chapter Three) were the only things that made the sound wave produced by one instrument sound different from the sound wave produced by another instrument. The difference between a guitar and a violin or between a trumpet and a saxophone was entirely a matter of the differing amplitudes of the overtones making up the sound—or so it was believed.

This theory turned out to be wrong. When scientists programmed computers to synthesize sound waves, they programmed them to produce the proper numbers to represent the fundamentals and overtones of several musical instruments. Yet when these numbers were converted into actual sounds with the aid of a digital-to-analog converter and an amplifier, they didn't sound right. They sounded phony, electronic; no one would have mistaken them for real musical instruments.

What went wrong? When these scientists studied the problem more closely, they realized that there was more to the sound of a musical instrument than just the fundamental tone and the overtones. To make the synthesized sounds more realistic, it was necessary to duplicate the envelope of the sound being synthesized.

The envelope of a sound is the amount of time it takes the sound to reach full volume and the way in which it falls off again to silence. The envelope of a sound is described fully by four values: the attack, the decay, the sustain, and the release, sometimes collectively abbreviated as ADSR. Each of these values can be represented as a number.

The attack is the amount of time it takes for a musical sound to rise to its loudest volume. The decay is the amount of time the sound takes to fall to its sustain level, which is the volume the musical sound remains at for most of the time it is being played. The release is the amount of time the sound takes to fall from its sustain level to total silence.

Taken together, the attack, decay, sustain, and release are said to constitute the shape of the envelope of the sound.

A digital synthesizer can duplicate the envelopes of most musical instruments or can create brand-new envelopes, for sounds that have never previously been heard by human ears.

In addition, most synthesizers allow the users to select from a number of wave forms. The wave form determines the way in which the sound wave rises and falls. A square wave, for instance, is a wave form that rises suddenly, remains at its highest level briefly, then falls off suddenly, giving it a "square" shape. A sawtooth wave form, on the other hand, rises steadily, then falls off just as steadily, giving it a jagged appearance resembling the cutting edge of a saw. Each waveform has its own characteristic sound.

The development of inexpensive microprocessors, tiny "computers on a chip," led to the development of inexpensive digital

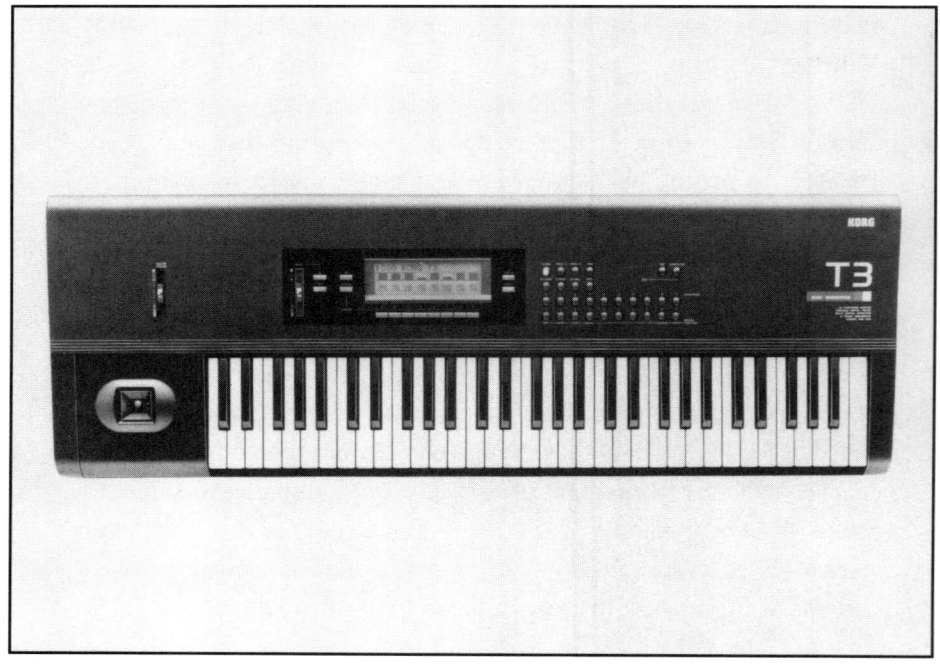

An example of a modern digital synthesizer. Portable, yet capable of an enormous variety of sounds and relatively inexpensive, synthesizers have become accessible to many more people than Robert Moog's original creation.

synthesizers in the 1980s. Although not as versatile and realistic-sounding as the synthesizers used by professional musicians, the low cost of these microprocessor-based synthesizers has helped them to find their way into many homes. Typically, these synthesizers feature pianolike keyboards along with switches that allow the user to change the nature of the sound produced by the synthesizer.

Furthermore, many of the home computers marketed in the 1980s sported synthesizer-like capabilities in addition to their other features, often at an amazingly low price. Some computers, for instance, include special processing circuitry that can generate a wide variety of wave forms and envelopes. Newer microcomputers (and synthesizers) use a more advanced method of music synthesis. The sounds of several musical instruments are stored in digital form in the computer's memory—the electronic circuits inside a computer that store information—as a series of binary numbers. The synthesizer chip included with these computers then manipulates these numbers to give the illusion that the recorded instrument is playing various musical notes, at different volumes. The result sounds amazingly like a real musical instrument.

Of course, a good synthesizer is not restricted to duplicating the sounds of musical instruments; other sounds can also be imitated. Computer-based synthesizers are called upon to generate a wide assortment of sounds, such as the sound of pistols being discharged or laser beams zapping spaceships. More and more, digital sound effects are used in movies and TV shows to produce sounds that would be impossible to create in any other manner, from the speech of alien beings to the noise made by futuristic machines and weapons.

Speech Synthesis
One form of nonmusical sound that computers are frequently called on to synthesize is the sound of the human voice. Speech synthesis allows computers to talk to users in normal-sounding (or nearly normal-sounding) human voices. If you have access to a personal

computer, you may have encountered programs that "speak" to you, often at surprising moments. Sometimes these voices are clear and audible; at other times, they are muddied and strangely accented. Familiar machines can suddenly talk. Vending machines recommend products or thank you for using them; automobiles remind you that the key is still in the ignition.

There are several ways to make a computer or other machine talk. The simplest, and the one used in most (though by no means all) personal computer programs, is to record the speech using standard digital recording techniques. The binary numbers representing the words to be spoken are stored in the computer's memory and are "played back" using some form of digital-to-analog conversion.

This is far and away the least versatile method of speech synthesis. The only speech that can be synthesized is the speech that was recorded. If the recorded speech consists of the words "Hello, my name is George," it can never be changed to say, "Hello, my name is Pete" or anything else.

A somewhat more versatile method of speech synthesis is word-based or phrase-based synthesis. This type involves recording certain words or phrases in digital form, then playing them back in various orders, so that a large variety of sentences can be synthesized. For instance, if you have recorded the words "the," "cat," "ate," and "plant," you can generate the sentences, "The cat ate the plant," and "The plant ate the cat," as well as such nonsense sentences as "Ate the cat plant," and "Plant the cat, ate."

If you then add the word "watched," you can generate the sentences, "The cat watched the plant," "The plant watched the cat," "Watched, the cat ate the plant," and so forth. The more words and phrases that you have recorded digitally, the more sentences the synthesizer can generate.

In many cities, the telephone company makes available a number that you can call to learn the current time. Readers who have called this number will have heard an example of phrase-based speech synthesis. Although it sounds like a real woman on the other end of the line reciting the time, it is actually a phrase-based synthesizer that contains a recording of the phrase, "At the tone, the time will be," along with recordings of the words "one," "two," "twenty," "thirty," "and," "seconds," and so forth. These are then combined by computer to form such sentences as, "At the tone, the time will be one-thirty-two and twenty seconds."

Many hand-held electronic toys, such as those used to teach young children to read and write, contain limited phrase-based synthesizers. Usually, these toys interact with the child by responding to the pressing of buttons or sensitive membranes representing words, letters of the alphabet, etc.

A phrase-based synthesizer that contained every word in the English language would be capable of generating every possible sentence in the English language. However, digital speech recordings take up a lot of space in a computer's memory. A recording of every word in the English language would require more memory than is available in the current generation of computers.

In addition, phrase-based synthesizers have a somewhat unrealistic sound because the spoken words have no inflection. Individual words are not given special emphasis. The sentences sound emotionless, and their precise meaning is often lost. Consider, for example, the sentence, "Is that your dog?" If the emphasis is placed on the word "that," then the question is asking whether this particular dog is your dog or if perhaps some other dog is your dog. If the emphasis is on the word "your," then the question is asking whether this is your dog or somebody else's dog. And if the emphasis is on the word "dog," then the question is asking whether this is your "dog" rather than your cat or your hamster. Phrase-based synthesizers cannot put this kind of emphasis on words.

The most versatile type of speech synthesizer is the phoneme-based synthesizer. A phoneme is the unit of speech much as the letter is the unit of written language. Every sound that your mouth is capable of creating is a phoneme. Every word or sentence that you speak is made up of some combination of these phonemes. In addition, most phonemes can be pronounced in several different ways. These variations on phonemes are called allophones.

A phoneme-based synthesizer contains actual digital recordings of all the phonemes used in the English language and all of the allophones of those phonemes. These can then be recombined to form words, sentences, entire speeches. A phoneme-based synthesizer can generate every possible sentence in the English language. However, it uses a small amount of computer memory compared to a phrase-based synthesizer because only the phonemes need to be recorded and not all possible words that can be made up from those phonemes. A phoneme-based synthesizer can even add inflection to give meaning to a sentence.

But phoneme-based synthesizers are also more difficult to create and use. And even the best phoneme-based synthesizers sound strange to the ear, as if the synthesizer spoke English with a foreign accent.

Phoneme-based synthesizers, in the form of computer programs, are available for most personal computers. At least one personal computer even has a phoneme-based synthesizer as part of its operating system (the program that is built into the computer before it is purchased).

Speech Recognition

The prospect of computers talking to their users is an enticing one. To some extent, of course, computers already can talk to their users, albeit in strange, difficult-to-understand accents. As methods of phoneme-based speech synthesis are improved, however, computers will become more and more articulate.

How much nicer still it would be if we could talk back to our computers! If you could give a computer a command simply by speaking to it, you wouldn't have to worry that you were a poor typist or that you weren't quite sure about how to spell a word. You could simply talk to the computer and the computer would understand.

Better still, you could use a computer as a kind of voice-operated typewriter. If you had a report due for school and wanted it neatly typed but didn't know how to use a keyboard, you could dictate it to the computer. The computer would then type it neatly on its printer, and your fingers would never have to touch the keys.

Not surprisingly, computer scientists have already experimented with speech recognition, the opposite of speech synthesis. But it's much harder to make a computer understand human speech than it is to make a computer speak.

How would you go about making a computer understand speech? Well, you could create a dictionary of digitized words, not unlike that used by a phrase-based speech synthesizer. The computer would then digitize (convert into numbers) the sound of your voice and compare it with its dictionary of digitized words. For instance, if you spoke the word "Hello," the computer would convert the word into a sequence of numbers and compare it against the numbers stored in its dictionary until it found a sequence that matched the word you had spoken.

The problem with this method is that no two people pronounce words in exactly the same way. Worse, the same person may pronounce the same word differently at different times. And most people run their words together when they speak, so that it is difficult for the computer to tell where one word ends and another begins.

The poor computer is unlikely ever to "hear" a sequence of numbers that matches one of the sequences in its dictionary.

What can be done? One trick is for the computer to search out sequences of numbers that are similar but not identical to the ones spoken by the user. But even this method is not enough to help a computer recognize words spoken by several different individuals. So most computer voice recognition systems have to be "taught" to recognize the speech of a particular user. The user must recite a series of words into a microphone, which are digitized by the computer and placed into its dictionary. When the user then talks to the computer, he or she must be careful to separate one word from the other.

We tend to think of our ears as being slightly less important than our eyes—a picture is worth a thousand words, the saying goes—but is this really true? It would seem that rays of light carry much more information than sound waves do, but the truth is that we can use sound waves in much the same way that we use light rays.

In effect, we can "see with sound." In the next chapter, we'll find out how.

7
Seeing With Sound

We see with light; we hear with sound. But light carries information differently from sound. Light bounces off objects, bringing us information about the surfaces of those objects that helps us locate things and find our way about. Sound, on the other hand, tells us mostly about things that vibrate.

Light can bounce off almost anything; relatively few things vibrate. Thus, light tells us about more things in the world around us than sound does.

But sound can bounce, too. When sound bounces, we call it an echo. You've probably heard echoes in confined places: shower stalls, empty rooms, rocky canyons. When a sound wave strikes the walls of such a confined place, it bounces (sometimes several times) and eventually returns to our ears.

Since sound waves bounce much as light does, can they carry information about surfaces just as light does? Can we "see" with sound? Can we use echoes to find our way about in the world?

Yes. The modern name for "seeing with sound" is sonar, which stands for **SO**und **NA**vigation and **R**anging. But sonar has been around for a long time. In fact, there are animals that can see better with sound than with light.

Natural Sonar

Natural sonar is also known as echolocation because it allows certain animals to locate things and find their way around using the echoes produced by sound waves.

Several animals, including several different types of birds, use echolocation in addition to (or as a replacement for) their powers of sight. The best known are the bats and porpoises.

Some (though not all) species of bats have poor eyesight; hence the expression, "blind as a bat," though bats are not totally blind. Because bats hunt for their food at night, they don't need good eyes because there is very little light to help them see. Instead, they use a form of sonar. They literally see with sound.

A typical species of bat makes a clicking sound with its tongue, then listens for the echo of this sound. If it hears an echo, it knows that there is a surface in the direction of the echo reflecting the sound wave. If it hears several echoes, it knows that there are several surfaces. If it hears no echo at all, it knows that there are only wide open spaces ahead.

Furthermore, the bat can tell how far away the surface is by timing how long it takes the echo to return to its ears. If the echo comes back almost immediately, the surface must be directly in front of it. If it comes back, say, half a second later, then the surface must be several hundred feet away.

If you've ever seen a bat fly, you know that it moves very quickly, darting about with a rapid swooping motion. Yet the bat sees its surroundings only through sonar. How can it learn enough about the world around it to avoid running into trees, buildings, people?

Amazingly, the bat can learn a great deal very quickly purely through sound. Some bats can emit as many as 200 clicks a second and can listen for the echoes from each.

The bat handles the information from these echoes in pretty much the same way that you handle the information from light. When you look around yourself, you don't consciously think about the many rays of light that went into producing the image of the world you see with your eyes. You don't measure the wavelength of each light ray to determine what color something is or the angle of a light ray to determine what direction it came from. There is a special part of your brain that is devoted to doing these very things, but you don't have to be aware that they are being done. The information in light is processed so automatically by your brain that you are not even aware of what is happening.

Dolphins are able to move rapidly through murky ocean water using sonar to locate obstacles.

There is a special part of the bat's brain that processes the information in echoes in much the same way that part of your brain processes the information in light. To a bat, seeing with sound is as natural as seeing with light is to a human being. Probably a bat sees an "image" in its brain produced by echoes much as you see an image in your brain produced by the light that strikes your eyes.

Porpoises, whales, and dolphins also use a form of echolocation to find their way around underwater. Dolphins, for instance, can make a clicking sound that sounds to human ears a little like the quacking of a duck. This sound bounces off underwater objects and allows the dolphin to steer itself rapidly through the murky world under the sea.

Artificial Sonar

Artificial, or man-made, sonar is a far more recent development than bat sonar. Bats have been around for millions of years. Man-made sonar has been around only since the 1930s.

Sonar was developed so that human beings could "see" in a realm where light rays generally do not go: the depths of the ocean. Light travels poorly through water. Dive far enough beneath the surface of the ocean and you will find yourself in a world as dark as night. Sound, on the other hand, travels easily through water. In fact, sounds travel more easily underwater than through the air. A sound that would travel only hundreds of feet through the air can travel many miles under the ocean.

Sonar was first used for depth finding. Ships need to know how deep a body of water is so as not to run aground. At one time, the only way to determine the depth was to lower an object into the water on a rope and measure how much rope had to be paid out before the object struck bottom.

With sonar, however, it is possible to tell the depth of a body of water by timing how long it takes a sound wave to echo back from the bottom. This is similar to the way in which you can tell how far away a lightning bolt is by timing how long it takes the thunder to arrive.

Depth finders based on sonar are now so common that you can buy them in any store that sells fishing gear.

During World War II, sonar was used to detect submarines underwater. In order to spot a submarine while it's submerged, a tight beam of sound waves is swept back and forth underwater, its echoes carefully timed. When an echo returns too quickly to have been reflected from the bottom (or when a new echo appears that had not been detected on a previous sweep), a submarine has probably been located.

How do we create a tight beam of sound waves? We saw in Chapter One that sound waves radiate outward in all directions from a vibrating object. How do we focus these rays into a single beam?

We do it by taking advantage of interference. When two or more sound waves come together, they interfere with one another. The crests of one sound wave cancel out the troughs of another to create sudden bursts of silence. By deliberately mixing sound waves together, we can cancel out parts of the sound wave completely, while making other parts even more intense. This is the method used to create a tightly aimed sonar beam.

The Sounds of War
A submarine is a kind of stealth boat. In times of war, it can slip into enemy territory almost completely undetected. Hidden by murky underwater shadows, it is nearly invisible.

But a submarine must be able to see, and those same underwater shadows that hide the submarine also render it blind. When it is underwater, sonar equipment becomes the "eyes" of the submarine. Tightly pulsed waves of sound allow the submarine not only to see where it is going, but to see other submarines and surface ships as well.

Important portions of World War II were fought underwater. Some experts believe that if there is another world war during the next few decades—a prospect that looks thankfully less likely due to political developments in the last few years—submarines will again play a key role. In an exchange of nuclear missiles, much will depend on the

Sonar is important in submarine navigation as well as defense. The USS *Newport News* is a nuclear-powered attack submarine.

missile-carrying submarines whose location cannot be known in advance by the enemy. And if there is no nuclear exchange, submarines may be vital in the defense of areas such as the Greenland-Iceland-United Kingdom (GIUK) gap, the sea route that separates the United Kingdom from the Soviet Union.

In a future submarine battle, sonar will play an important role in underwater strategy. But using sonar to detect enemy submarines and other underwater hazards isn't as simple as it might sound.

The path of a sound wave underwater is rarely straight and true. Earlier, we saw that changes in air temperature can change the direction of a sound wave, causing it to curve up or down or even sideways. The same is true of a sonar beam underwater. As the water that the beam is passing through changes temperature, the beam changes direction. A beam passing from warmer water into cooler water, for instance, will tend to curve in the direction of the cooler water, and a beam passing from cooler into warmer water will curve in the direction of the warmer water. Since water normally becomes cooler with greater depth, a sonar beam moving downward will tend to curve ever more steeply downward, and a beam moving upward will tend to curve ever more steeply upward.

The same thing happens when water pressure changes, but the results are often the reverse of those described in the last paragraph, since the sonar beam tends to curve away from greater pressure. Water pressures increase with depth, so a sonar beam moving downward will actually tend to curve back upward. When we combine the effects of changing temperature and pressure, we discover that a sonar beam moving downward will at first curve more steeply downward, then will curve back upward again in a long arc until it finally comes back to the surface—often as much as thirty miles from the submarine producing the beam.

A sonar beam striking the surface of the water from below, however, tends to bounce right back down into the depths, so the process described above can actually repeat itself over and over again, with the sonar beam going down and back up, down and back up, down and back up, in a series of sweeping arcs.

Thus, it is actually possible for a submarine to send a sonar beam many tens and even hundreds of miles away, detecting objects on the surface at distances of quite a few miles. Alas, because of the way the beam arcs downward and returns to the surface, there are quite a few blind spots in the submarine's ability to see with sound.

So complicated are the ways in which sonar beams behave underwater that the returning signals have to be analyzed by computer before their meaning can be fully deciphered. It may take many minutes and many sonar blips before ships and other submarines can be accurately detected. The degree of accuracy associated with a sonar signal is sometimes called the solution and is measured in percentages. A 99 percent solution would indicate that the information calculated from the sonar signal has a 99 percent chance of being accurate, while a 10 percent solution would have only a 10 percent chance of being accurate.

The sonar apparatus is commonly built right into the hull of the submarine. But hull sonars can't see behind the submarine in an area known as the baffles, where the propellers distort the signal. And they can't operate at all when the submarine is going fast because the sound of flowing water drowns out the sonar signal. Many submarines, therefore, tow their sonar apparatuses behind them in a formation known as a towed array, which is less subject to this kind of interference.

The greatest drawback of sonar is that it makes noise. Sonar helps a submarine to detect other submarines, but it also announces the presence of the submarine itself. Other submarines or surface ships can hear the sonar blips and use them to locate the submarine producing the beam. A submarine that does not wish to be detected will either not use sonar at all or will use it only briefly. Instead, the commander of the submarine may choose to listen for sounds produced by other ships, a system sometimes called passive sonar. (A ship sending out a sonar beam is said to be using active sonar.)

Even helicopters can use sonar to detect submarines. There are two methods that can be employed. The helicopter can hover near the surface of the ocean and dip a sonar apparatus into the water. Or it can drop a sonobouy, which floats in the water, sending sonar beams into the depths and broadcasting the resulting signals back to the helicopter via short-range radio.

Ultrasound

A major problem with "seeing" with sound is the size of the sound waves. Their wavelengths are large because the larger the wavelength, the less we can see when those waves bounce off a surface. Waves of light have extremely small wavelengths compared to those of a typical sound wave, which is why they are ideal for seeing. Sound waves in the range that human beings can hear, on the other hand, are much too large to detect tiny surfaces or tiny details in a surface.

Sound waves that are too high-pitched for human beings to hear, however, have shorter wavelengths than do sound waves that can be heard. These ultrasonic sounds are sometimes called ultrasound—literally, "beyond sound." Ultrasound can be used to produce "pictures" much more detailed than can be produced with the sound waves that we can hear.

Sonar uses ultrasonic sound waves to detect underwater objects. But ultrasound can be used to see things in places other than the ocean. For instance, it can be used to look inside the human body.

When we use ultrasound to look inside the body, we are using it in a role traditionally played by X-rays. X-rays are a form of electromagnetic radiation with extremely short wavelengths. Because of these short wavelengths, X-rays can go places that ordinary light rays cannot go. However, because they pack a great deal of energy inside their short waves, X-rays can sometimes cause damage. Brief exposure to X-rays, such as in a dentist's office, are usually harmless. But prolonged exposure can cause tissue damage that can lead to cancer. And pregnant women should avoid X-rays, because they can harm their unborn children.

Low-energy ultrasound is often used as an alternative to X-rays because it is believed to be safer. However, little is known about the long-term effects of exposure to ultrasound, so it is used sparingly.

When ultrasound waves pass through the human body, they are reflected by changes in density within the body. Therefore they give us information about bones and tissues inside the body. A typical use for ultrasound is in examining a fetus in a pregnant woman's womb. The "picture" produced by the ultrasound examination can tell a doctor approximately how long it will be before the child is born, whether the child is suffering from obvious physical problems, and whether the child will be a boy or a girl.

In addition to exploring the human body, ultrasound can be used to test metal objects. When ultrasound passes through a metal, it is reflected by cracks and small defects; thus, it can be used to map or to reveal the presence of such imperfections.

It isn't easy to generate an ultrasonic sound wave. One way in which it can be done is with the aid of piezoelectricity, which is a form of electricity that is created when certain crystals or ceramics are exposed to ordinary electricity. A crystal or ceramic plate will begin to vibrate when electricity is passed through it in such a way that the electric current rapidly alternates, that is, changes direction. The frequency with which the current changes direction determines the frequency of the vibration. If the alternation is rapid enough, the vibrating plate will produce an ultrasonic wave.

Ultrasound at Work

Ultrasound is good for other things besides "seeing." High energy ultrasound can shake dirt off metal, for instance. This process is called ultrasonic cleaning.

The secret behind this use of ultrasound is a process called cavitation. When high-energy ultrasound waves pass through water, they can actually "tear" the water apart. Tiny holes or cavities appear briefly in the water, then collapse. When these cavities collapse, they release surprisingly large amounts of energy in the form of heat, almost like miniature explosions. Some of these collapsing cavities are briefly as hot as the surface of the sun. Fortunately, they are also very small, so this heat can be quickly absorbed by the comparatively large amounts of surrounding water.

The shock waves produced in the water by cavitation have a powerful agitating effect on objects submerged in the water and can rattle dirt and other foreign objects off a piece of metal quite rapidly and thoroughly.

Ultrasonic shock waves can also be used to mix together liquids that would not ordinarily combine. The old saying has it that "oil and water don't mix." Ordinarily this statement is true, but ultrasound can break oil, water, and other nonmixing liquids into fragments that will mix together. This process is used to produce such consumer products as peanut butter, mayonnaise, and floor polish.

The heat released by cavitation is also valuable in promoting certain chemical processes. Ultrasound is used in a number of manufacturing processes involving chemical reactions.

The world would be a poor place without sound. Although silence can be enjoyable in its own right, the sounds of music, laughter, interesting speech, sound effects, etc., are a delight as well.

In this book, we hope you've learned things about sound that you've never known before: how it is created, how it can be recorded and transmitted, how it can be used to see and even to clean. The sounds that reach our ear are only a small part of the exciting world of sound.

Glossary

aliasing—A phenomenon by which a high-pitched sound wave in a digital recording can sound like a low-pitched hum during playback.

allophones—The different ways in which a single phoneme can be pronounced.

amplitude—The difference in height from a wave's crest to its trough.

amplitude modulation—The process of adding information to a wave by changing the amplitude of the wave in a pattern; AM, for short.

analog—A form of information recording and transmission that uses a representation, or analog, that is in some way like the original information.

analog-to-digital converter—A device for translating an analog information representation to a digital information representation.

attack—The time that it takes for a musical sound to rise to its full volume.

atoms—The extremely tiny particles that make up all matter.

auditory ossicles—The bones in the middle ear that carry sound vibration from the eardrum to the inner ear.

bel—The basic unit for measuring sound, though the *decibel* (one-tenth of a bel) is more commonly used.

binary number—A numbering system that represents all numbers using only the digits 0 and 1.

binaural—Word used to describe the process of hearing with two ears, which allows us to identify the direction from which a sound is coming.

cassette recorder—Tape recorder in which the tape is placed in a small plastic cassette.

cavitation—Heat released by the collapse of tiny bubbles created by the passage of sound through water.

channel codes—The special number codes used to store binary numbers on the surface of a compact disc.

communication—The transmission of information from one individual to another.

compact disc—A disc with a silvered surface in which pits have been dug to represent sound waves.

compression waves—A wave in which the crests are compressed regions of a substance such as air and the troughs are uncompressed regions of that substance, moving in a pattern.

conductor—A substance through which electricity can flow.

crest—The highest point of a wave.

cycle—The entire wave from one crest to the next.

decay—The amount of time that it takes a musical note to fall from its full volume to its *sustain* level.

decibel—One tenth of a *bel*.

decimal numbers—A numbering system that represents all numbers using the digits 0, 1, 2, 3, 4, 5, 6, 7, 8 ,9.

depth finding—The use of sonar to determine ocean depths.

diaphragm—A thin plate or membrane that vibrates when struck by sound waves.

digital audio tape—Magnetic tape used to record sound in digital form.

digital recording—Sound recording methods that represent sounds as sequences of numbers.

digital-to-analog converter (DAC)—Device for converting information from digital form into an analog form.

Doppler effect—The phenomenon, named for Austrian physicist Christian Doppler, by which sounds produced by an object moving toward you seem to have a higher pitch than normal and sounds produced by an object moving away from you seem to have a lower pitch than normal.

eardrum—The taut, flat membrane of skin between the outer and inner ears that vibrates when sound waves strike it; also called the *tympanic membrane*.

earflap—The shell-shaped piece of skin attached to the side of the head; part of the outer ear.

echolocation—A natural form of sonar found in some animals.

electricity—The flow of electrons through a substance called a conductor.

electromagnetic—A form of wave that travels through space itself and can be used to carry information. Light is a form of electromagnetic radiation, as are radio waves, X-rays and gamma rays.

electrons—Particles smaller than atoms.

emulsion—Semi-liquid substance used to coat the surface of magnetic recording media, usually containing microscopic magnetic particles.

envelope—The shape of a musical sound, consisting of the *attack*, *decay*, *sustain*, and *release*.

error correction codes—Special codes used in digital recordings that allow errors in the recording to be corrected during playback.

frequency—The number of wave crests that pass a given point in one second.

fundamental—The lowest frequency sound wave produced by a musical instrument.

gramophone—The original type of phonograph invented by Thomas Edison, which recorded sound as grooves on the surface of a cylinder.

hertz (hz)—The frequency of a wave described as the number of cycles to pass a given point in one second.

infrasonic—Word used to describe sounds that have frequencies too low to be heard by the human ear.

inner ear—The portion of the ear where sound is converted into electrical and chemical signals that travel to the brain.

kinetic energy—Energy possessed by an object in motion.

lands—The silvered areas between the holes (or *pits*) in the surface of a compact disc.

larynx—The organ in the human throat that contains the vocal cords.

loudness—The characteristic of sound that is determined by the amplitude of the sound wave.

magnetic tape—Tape coated with magnetic emulsion, used to record sound.

meatus—The passageway inside your earflap leading to the eardrum.

media—The various physical forms in which information, such as sound, can be recorded; plural of *medium*.

memory—The portion of a computer where information is stored while not actually being processed.

microphone—A device for converting soundwaves into electrical signals.

microprocessor—A small, silicon-based chip containing all or most of the circuitry necessary for a computer to perform computations.

middle ear—The portion of the ear just inside the eardrum.

modem—Device for converting digital information into tones that can be transmitted over a telephone; short for modulator-demodulator.

modulation—The process of adding information to a wave.

molecules—Chains of atoms.

morse code—A code that allows information to be sent over a telegraph or similar device as a series of long and short pulses, called dots and dashes.

outer ear—The part of the ear that is visible on the outside of your head.

overtime—Sound waves produced by a musical instrument that have frequencies that are multiples of the fundamental.

passive sonar—The process of detecting ships and submarines by the sounds that they make.

phoneme—A unit of speech.

phoneme-based synthesis—Speech synthesis that used the individual sounds of human speech, or *phonemes*, and places them into the appropriate order under the control of a computer.

phonetic alphabet—A specially-designed alphabet in which each character corresponds to one and only one speech sound.

phonograph—A device for recording sounds as grooves on the surface of a disc or a cylinder.

pitch—The characteristic of sound that is determined by the frequency of the sound wave.

pits—Tiny holes in the silvered surface of a compact disc.

potential energy—Energy possessed by an object that is not currently moving, but that can start moving with a minimum of effort.

radiate—To move outward in all directions.

radio—A device for transmitting sound in the form of electromagnetic radiation.

reel-to-reel tape recorder—Tape recorder in which the tape is placed on two physically separate reels.

release—The amount of time that it takes for a musical sound to fall from its *sustain* level to total silence.

resonance—The phenomenon by which a sound or other vibration can cause other objects to vibrate.

reverberation—The echoing of a sound in a confined place that can make it seem fuller and richer.

sampling rate—The number of times that a digital recording device measures the amplitude of a sound wave every second.

sine wave—A wave that rises and falls in a simple, repetitive pattern.

solution—The reliability of a sonar signal detecting a ship or submarine.

sonar—A device for detecting surfaces at a distance by bouncing sound waves off of them and listening to the echoes; short for **SO**und **NA**vigation and **R**anging.

sonic boom—Loud sound wave created by an object moving faster than the speed of sound.

sound synthesis—The process of mechanically or electronically creating sounds that do not necessarily exist in nature.

spark gap—A gap in an electric circuit across which electric current can jump in abrupt sparks.

speech—The form of communication, used only (as far as we know) by human beings, that involves making meaningful sounds with the mouth and larynx.

speech center—The part of the brain that controls the production of speech.

speech recognition—The process, only crudely developed at present, by which a computer can "understand" and interpret human speech.

speech synthesis—The process by which a computer or computer-based device can produce artificial human speech.

supersonic—Moving at speeds greater than that of sound.

sustain—The volume at which a musical note remains for most of its duration, after falling from its maximum volume.

tape recorder—Device for recording sounds on magnetic tape.

telegraph—A device for transmitting electrical pulses over a wire to carry information; literally, "writing at a distance."

telephone—A device for transmitting sound in the form of electrical signals over a wire; literally, "sound at a distance."

timbre—The sound quality produced by a combination of a fundamental sound wave and its overtones; also called *tone color*.

tone color—See *timbre*.

towed array—A sonar device towed behind a submarine, where it will not be confused by engine noises.

transverse waves—Waves that vibrate back and forth in a direction different to the one in which they are traveling.

trough—The lowest point of a wave.

tympanic membrane—See *inner ear*.

ultrasonic—Word used to describe sounds that have frequencies too high to be heard by the human ear.

ultrasound—High frequency sound waves used to examine the insides of opaque objects such as the human body, or to clean dirt off of surfaces.

vibration—A rhythmic motion that can create a wave.

vinyl—All-purpose name for the plastic substances used to produce traditional LPs.

vision—The process of detecting and decoding the information contained in visible light.

wave—A rhythmic motion that travels through a medium such as air or water, carrying energy with it.

wave form—The way in which a sound waves rises and falls.

wave interference—The combining of two waves to form a wave with the attributes of both.

wavelength—The distance from crest to crest (or trough to trough) of a wave.

word-based synthesis—Speech synthesis that utilizes prerecorded words that can be placed in the appropriate order by a computer.

Further Reading

Alkin, Glyn. *Sound Recording and Reproduction*. Focal Press: Stoneham, Mass., 1987.

Cousins, Margaret. *The Story of Thomas Alva Edison*. Random House: New York, 1981.

Kavaler, Lucy. *The Dangers of Noise*. Crowell: New York, 1978.

Lampton, Christopher F. *Thomas Alva Edison*. Franklin Watts: New York, 1988.

Pelta, Kathy. *Alexander Graham Bell*. Silver-Burdett: Englewood Cliffs, N.J., 1989.

Silverstein, Alvin and Virginia B. *The Story of Your Ear*. Coward-McCann: New York, 1981.

Ward, Brian. *The Ear and Hearing*. Franklin Watts: New York, 1981.

Waterman, Talbot H. *Animal Navigation*. Scientific American Library: New York, 1988.

Wicks, Keith. *Sound and Recording*. Franklin Watts: New York, 1982.

Index

A ADSR, 69
amplitude, 12, 15, 22–23
modulation (AM), 48
analog recording, 57
analog-to-digital converter (ADC), 58–60
antennae, 48
attack, 69
auditory ossicles, 21

B bats, 78–80
bel (measurement), 23
Bell, Alexander G., 23, 44
Berliner, Emile, 53
binary numbers, 59
binaural hearing, 22
broadcasting, radio, 49–50

C cassette tape, 55–56, 62
cavitation, 87
channel codes, 60–61, 62
communication, 31
compact discs, 56–63
computers, 59–61, 63
consonants, 33–34
crest (of a wave), 10–12

D decay, 69
digital recording, 57–66
digital-to-analog converter (DAC), 61
decibel, 23
depth-finding, 80–81
diaphragm, 45, 51–52
digital audio tape (DAT), 64–66
Doppler, Christian, 26
doppler effect, 25–27

E ear, 19–22, 24
inner, 21–22
middle, 20–21
outer, 19–20
eardrums, 20–21
earflaps, 19
Edison, Thomas A., 44, 51–54
echolocation, 78–80
electricity, 9, 41–42, 44–46, 48, 54, 58–59, 61
electromagnetic radiation, 46–48
electrons, 9, 41
energy, 9–11, 22–24, 40
error correction codes, 62

F fenestra ovalis, 21
Fessenden, Reginald, 48
frequency, 11, 15, 24–25
fundamental, 36

H hearing, 19–29
damage to, 37–39
Henry, Joseph, 41–42
Hertz, Heinrich, 11, 47
hertz (hz), 11

I incus, 20–21
information, 30–39, 41–50
infrasonic, 25
Integrated Services Digital Network (ISDN), 63–64
interference, 12

K kinetic energy, 9–11, 13–14, 41

L lands, 60
larynx, 32
laser beams, 60
loudness, 22–24, 40
loudspeaker, 46

M Marconi, M.G., 46–47, 49
meatus, 19

microphone, 44–46
microprocessors, 70–71
Moog, Robert, 68
Moog synthesizer, 68, 70
morse code, 42, 48
Morse, Samuel, 41–43
music, 35–36, 39
    synthesis, 68–71

N needle, phonograph, 51–53
networks, radio, 50
noise, 36–39

O oval window, 21
overtones, 36, 69

P phonemes, 73–74
phonetic alphabet, 34
phonograph, 51–54
pitch, 24–27
pits, 60
potential energy, 9–10, 13–14

R radio, 46–50
receivers, radio, 48
reel-to-reel tape, 55–56
release, 69
resonance, 27–29
reverberation, 28–29

S sampling rate, 59–60, 65
sawtooth wave, 70
sight, 8, 77–78
SONAR (sound navigation and
    ranging), 78–85
  active, 85
  passive, 84–85
  solution of, 84
sonic boom, 17
sonobuoy, 85
sound
  and information, 30–39
  carried by electricity, 41–46
  defined, 9
  envelope, 69–70
  recording of, 51–66

speed of, 15–17
synthesis, 67–76
waves, 12–15, 35–36, 45, 68–71
sound barrier, breaking of, 16–17
speech, 31–35
    computer recognition of, 74–76
    synthesis of, 71–74
speech center (brain), 31
square wave, 70
submarines, 81–85
supersonic aircraft, 16
sustain, 69
synthesizers, 68–71

T tape, magnetic, 54–56
telecommunication, 39–50
telegraph, 41–43
telephones, 44–46
    digital, 63–64
temperature, 15–16
    inversion, 16
timbre, 36
Titanic, HMS, 49–50
tone color, 36
towed array, 84
trough, 10–12
tuning fork, 35

U ultrasonic, 25
    cleaning, 86
ultrasound, 85–87

V vibration, 13, 20–21, 25
vocal cords, 25, 32
vowel, 34

W wave forms, 70
wave interference, 12
wavelength, 11, 15, 24–27
    of electromagnetic radiation, 47
waves, 9–15, 46–47